They had come here to begin to finalize the end of their marriage.

And somehow he was now holding her, his arm secured around her back and their bodies pressed close. He turned them and walked her back toward the large, comfortable bed a few feet away.

Zaynab gasped when the backs of her legs contacted the bed and gave way, bending, bowing, sending her reeling onto the cushioned support of the bed comforter and mattress. Ara followed her, his hands pressed by the sides of her head, their chests no longer touching and yet both matched in their heaving breathlessness.

Her eyes, still rounded with shocked confusion, flashed with a newer emotion. Desire, he recognized quickly, feeling the same yearning pump molten heat through his own body.

"I'm just making sure that we're both certain this is what we want." Ara took her chin in his hand again, his face lowering closer to hers until he could feel her sweet, warm breath stirring over his lips. "I can't walk away with any doubts. Can you?"

Dear Reader,

I know I'm not alone when I say that some of the best romance stories feature second chances!

The pining and longing, the unresolved feelings, and don't even get me started on the sparking chemistry. And who doesn't love a good grovel scene? *swoon*

Of course, before second chances happen, a little soul-searching, some self-evaluation and self-forgiveness have to come first. I thought about that a lot while writing Zaynab and Ara's story in *Another Shot at Forever*. Although their marriage isn't looking so good at the beginning, when a certain circumstance—surprise baby news!—brings them back together, Zaynab and Ara are given another chance that neither of them is prepared for at first.

It doesn't help that they couldn't be more different— Zaynab being cheerful and Ara with his whole broody aura. Yet they peel back the layers of their hearts, reveal their vulnerabilities and soon learn to trust each other. And though saving their marriage isn't the goal, somewhere along the way it grows into a possibility for them.

Now, whether it blossoms into a happily-ever-after...? Well, you'll have to read on to find out. ;)

Happy reading!

Hana

ANOTHER SHOT AT FOREVER

HANA SHEIK

ROMANCE

Harlequin® ROMANCE

ISBN-13: 978-1-335-21631-1

Another Shot at Forever

Harlequin Enterprises ULC
22 Adelaide St. West, 41st Floor
Toronto, Ontario M5H 4E3, Canada
www.Harlequin.com

Printed in U.S.A.

Recycling programs for this product may not exist in your area.

Hana Sheik falls in love every day reading her favorite romances and writing her own happily-ever-afters. She's worked various jobs—but never for very long because she's always wanted to be a romance author. Now she gets to happily live that dream. Born in Somalia, she moved to Ottawa, Canada, at a very young age and still resides there with her family.

Books by Hana Sheik

Harlequin Romance

Second Chance to Wear His Ring
Temptation in Istanbul
Forbidden Kisses with Her Millionaire Boss
The Baby Swap That Bound Them
Falling for Her Forbidden Bodyguard

Visit the Author Profile page at Harlequin.com.

Every writer knows writing is tough sometimes.
So, this one is for me.

Praise for
Hana Sheik

"*Second Chance to Wear His Ring* is so much
more than a typical romance story. It is a story of
overcoming personal tragedy and also has
huge cultural references!"

CHAPTER ONE

ZAYNAB SIRAD NEVER intended to divorce her husband at his sister's engagement party, and yet that was exactly what she planned to do when she showed up and proverbially darkened his doorstep with the impending news.

If there was ever a time for her to rethink her plan to serve him the papers, now was it.

It wasn't helping her resolve that the pleasant sounds of the party on the roof terrace drifted down to where she stood at the front entrance. She hadn't known there was a party happening until the guards at the front gate had informed her. Behind her the taxi she'd taken idled on the front drive alongside a number of other vehicles—her first indication that she'd have an audience for what she was about to do.

While one part of Zaynab squawked that she should come back at a later date when she could end this quietly, the part of her that had been waiting and dreading this moment for a little over a year now kept her feet rooted and straightened her shoulders.

I have to do this now. I've waited long enough. We both have...

Ignoring the wobble to her legs and the swooshing upheaval of her stomach, she stepped forward and grasped one of the polished silver handles of the large two-door entrance. Without delay Zaynab pulled open the door, passed hurriedly inside, and hadn't realized she'd been holding her breath until she released it when the front door clicked closed loudly behind her. "There's no going back now," she muttered under her breath.

Despite knowing that the hardest part still awaited her, taking this first step was a small victory of its own. And right now she needed to reward the small wins to steel her courage and banish her growing anxiety.

Swallowing past the anxious knot lodged in her throat, Zaynab turned to face the home that had never felt like hers in spite of being married to its owner and technically being the house's mistress.

Everything in the foyer looked the same bar the addition of the glittery ribbon and bright sweet-smelling flowers festooning the gleaming black banister of the staircase. Two dour-faced guards, hands poised behind their backs, stood fixed to their positions, one near the base of the stairs and the other at the top, their eyes tracking her as she walked toward the stairs. As always her gaze briefly dipped to the guns holstered at their waist belts, a new kind of nervous flutter working up her esophagus at the sight of the weaponry.

But aside from staring her down, the guards made no moves to deter her advance forward. Relieved, Zaynab surmised that they must have been informed of her arrival and clearance by the security personnel standing guard outdoors. It was one less thing she had to worry herself about.

I already have enough on my plate.

"You can do this," she quietly rallied herself.

Gathering her long black skirt and abaya up in one hand, she clutched the handrail and climbed the staircase to meet her fate.

She needn't have asked the guards for directions as she passed a few more on her way up the second flight of stairs to the third floor. String music, chatter and laughter from the party carried louder now. With this many people in one place, security had to be a top priority to the homeowner—her husband.

The man she'd come to divorce.

"You got this. Just walk right up to him, look him in the eyes and say, 'I want a divorce.'" It

sounded simple enough to her as she repeated
the course of action, but as boldly as Zaynab
entered the house initially, her trembling hand
betrayed her when she opened the door to the
terrace far more cautiously. Because now there
was only this last obstacle she had to pass. And
it wasn't much of a deterrent as the door easily
unlatched and opened.

The first thing to greet her besides the now
unfiltered noises of the party was the stun-
ningly bright light of day as she crossed the
threshold and closed the terrace door behind
her, her eyes having adjusted to the darker in-
terior of the house. Then after blinking several times and growing used to the daylight,
she took in the sight before her with a slack-
ened jaw.

Though she'd been up on the terrace before,
it might as well have been her first visit because
it looked like a whole different place.

Strung with a canopy of fairy lights and silky
silver drapes, the whitewashed posts formed
a long overhead trellis that led from the door
to the far edge of the roof. Zaynab tilted her
head up and surveyed the transformed setting,
her awe multiplying as she walked into the
party and took in all the beautiful changes to
the scenery. Gone were the wraparound teak
sofa with its colorful cushions, the large pot-

ted palms and the fire table, all replaced by long, shining white oak tables, sturdy cushioned benches and a large dais where a band was playing live music, the fluted notes of a wind instrument blending with the brisk keystrokes from the piano as a lively song matched the general mood of the party.

Each table was adorned by simple but elegant greenery, more string lights and candle votives. The table settings were untouched, a clue that the party must have only just begun since the guests hadn't dined yet. That knowledge gave her hope that maybe she could complete what she'd come to do without garnering too much attention. Still, her stomach churned when she walked a little farther onto the terrace and deeper into the party. Guests milled around the tables, some seated, everyone spread out and clustered into groups. From the looks of it, no one had come alone.

Except for me.

It dawned on her that she stood out like a sore thumb.

And she wasn't alone in noticing that she was an outlier. A few guests caught her eye, their curiosity clear in their lingering stares and furrowed brows. Was it her imagination or did their lips move faster as they watched her? Were they talking about her, wondering what she was possibly doing there?

Or perhaps they could sense that unlike them, she had no official invite. Not from the bride-to-be, or her groom, and not even from the party's host—her husband.

Well, *her husband* until she handed him the folded papers inside of her shoulder purse.

Thinking of the divorce she'd come for slowed her racing heart rate and calmed her mind a little. She had a reason to be here, though for a different reason than everyone else. And even though it wasn't the most opportune of settings, she would try very hard not to ruin the party for anyone. Zaynab was determined as ever, despite being in the company of strangers, to meet with her husband and do what she should have done a year ago.

Divorce him.

End their farce of a marriage and move past this stage of her life finally.

Zaynab searched the faces in the crowd, certain he'd be there. Somewhere. He was throwing the party for his sister's engagement after all. She grew frustrated when she didn't spot him. Walking and scouring the crush of guests, she smiled awkwardly a few times when she snagged more curious looks from these strangers. One of them was a pale-haired white woman, her chin-length bob a blond so icy it bordered on colorless. Despite her frosty coloring, her eyes were shining pools of hazel warmth and her smile invited Zaynab to slow and stop beside her.

"Hello, newcomer," the woman greeted her cheerfully, peeling herself out from under the arm of a lanky dark-haired young man who flashed Zaynab a grin. "If you're worried that you missed anything, don't be. Lunch hasn't begun, and no one's given speeches yet." The woman raised a champagne flute to her with a widening smile. "Are you with the bride-to-be or the groom-to-be?"

"Um, neither actually." Zaynab watched as the woman's smile flipped downward and confusion pinched the space between fine ash-blond brows. "I'm looking for...the host."

My husband was on the tip of her tongue, but that would require a long-winded explanation and she wasn't in the mood to divulge.

"Ara?"

Zaynab tensed up, her body freezing at the sound of his name as it always seemed to do these days. She forced herself to nod and watched as the woman tapped a long manicured nail at her chin thoughtfully.

"I arrived a lot earlier than everyone, and I definitely saw him then, but not since."

"Oh... I was hoping to speak with him."

Smiling, the woman held up a finger to her and turned to regard her companion. "Lucas, did you see where Ara went?"

"Who?" the dark-haired young man said, his head swiveling to them from the conversation he'd been having with another couple.

"Ara. You know, Anisa's older brother."

Anisa. Another name Zaynab hadn't heard in a while. She hadn't met Anisa officially yet, and given her reason for being there, she hoped to avoid a run-in with the bride-to-be at all costs.

"Well, why didn't you just say that, Darya?" Lucas scratched the scruffy beard at his cheek, hemming and hawing comically before he finally shook his head. "Nah, I don't remember. He's probably around though."

Zaynab could only pray that he was. Seeing as they couldn't help her, she thanked Darya and Lucas and walked away.

She didn't get far before she heard someone calling for Anisa.

It wasn't hard to tell who the bride-to-be was, as she was dressed in a white, gold-threaded guuntino, the traditional body-hugging outfit a favorite among Somali brides. And if her lovely dress wasn't a giveaway, Anisa's smile radiated an effulgent glow that spoke of her upcoming nuptials and future bliss.

Zaynab immediately recognized it because *she* had glowed just like that with the brilliant hope of what her married life would be like. Sadly, that spark in her was quickly snuffed out by the coldly cruel reality of her unhappy marriage.

Shaking away her depressive thoughts, she moved back into the crowd and studied Anisa from a safe distance.

Trailing behind her in a tan suit, with his gaze firmly glued to Anisa was a man Zaynab recognized more readily. Nasser, though she hadn't seen him for some time. Nasser worked in the private security sector where he ran his own company, and Ara had hired his services some time before Zaynab and he had married. She'd only met him once but that didn't stop her from being surprised that he was Anisa's chosen life partner. From her recollection, Nasser was similar to Ara in that he was frigidly taciturn and not at all easily approachable. But she wouldn't have been able to tell, not by the way he stared at Anisa. All she saw now was an unmasked abundance of love for his intended bride.

Impressive. I guess love does have some wonders, Zaynab mused.

Nasser palmed his clean-shaven jaw sheepishly as he joined Anisa in standing before an elderly couple. Judging by the way Anisa and Nasser shared similar embarrassed expressions, it seemed that they had been caught doing something they shouldn't have been doing together. They were quickly forgiven, as the older woman and man embraced them both.

Zaynab presumed they had to be Nasser's parents. They couldn't be Anisa's. She might not have been able to get Ara to open up about himself much, but it was common knowledge that both he and his younger sister had lost their parents in a tragic boating accident.

Though her marriage to him might be ending very soon, it didn't stop Zaynab's heart from panging in sorrow for Ara's loss. She couldn't fathom what it was like to lose one's parents so very young. She'd hoped secretly that she could fill that void and be his family once they married, but now all Zaynab desired was for their divorce to be filed and eventually finalized.

It was why she kept an eye on Anisa and Nasser. Surely Ara wouldn't be too far from his sister and future brother-in-law.

Where are you?

Biding her time wasn't working well. Anisa and Nasser mingled with his family some more before chatting with their guests and doing the circuit. Zaynab found a corner to avoid a meeting with them and pulled out her phone, resorting to messaging Ara since she couldn't track him down.

I'm here, at the house. I was hoping we could talk...

She thumbed the send button before she wimped out.

Staring up from her phone and looking around, she felt a fresh wave of exasperation and dread when Anisa and Nasser stopped to talk to the blond-haired Darya. Their chat was animated, laughter and gesturing relaxed as if the trio knew each other well. Worried that she would be mentioned, Zaynab backed toward the exit, pasting on a smile and praying she would make it without a confrontation.

As she did, she sent another message to Ara.

Leaving. Meet me at my hotel.

Sharing the pinned location of her hotel and feeling like she was far enough to safely turn her back on the party and make her hasty exit, Zaynab whipped around only to slam into a hard, warm wall. A wall that expelled an indignant huff upon contact and had big hands that quickly and firmly locked around her shoulders.

"Zaynab," the wall said her name in a huskily

deep, familiar voice that had her heart thundering from one breath to another and her head swirling with a number of emotions from apprehension to breathless anticipation.

She'd been looking for Ara all this time and now that he was in front of her, she didn't know what to say. Didn't even think she could move out of his grasp.

"Security informed me that you had arrived," he said as way of explanation.

"I…" She struggled to speak and realized it wasn't helping that his hands were still on her. Shrugging his touch off, she continued, "Yes, I didn't want to pull you away and decided to come up and look for you, but I couldn't find you."

"We must have missed each other then."

Zaynab couldn't understand how she could've missed him, but now that her eyes alighted on his figure, she knew why he hadn't jumped out to her immediately. First, he wasn't dressed in his usual business attire, and his choice of a polo shirt, chinos and high-top sneakers threw her for a loop. But more disconcerting than his atypical outfit was the warm smile he cast to a guest that called his name. Raising his hand in greeting, he gripped her wrist lightly with the other hand and tugged her after him.

"We need to talk," Zaynab told him.

"Not here," was his curt reply before Ara drew her after him gently, away from the merriment that was his sister's engagement party.

Running into his estranged wife at Anisa and Nasser's engagement party was a security measure Ara hadn't even thought to consider.

And why would he? They technically hadn't seen each other face-to-face for a year. Any communication they'd had since Zaynab left him to return to her home in London was short and infrequent. He counted a total of three brief calls with her. The first call had been shortly after she left, and he'd inquired about her safe landing, while the second call came from her a few days later. When he'd answered her call, she'd quickly explained that she hadn't meant to call him at all but that she'd made a mistake.

Admittedly that had stung him far more than he anticipated.

But as fragile as his ego was after that, it was the third call that lingered in his mind. The last one before they went a year's stretch without speaking.

When she called and asked for a divorce.

His jaw clenched at the memory.

Though it shouldn't have surprised him when she asked. After all, they had been married for a couple months at that point but they were virtual strangers. More than anything the fault was his. He hadn't known how to be a husband to her, to love and value her the way she deserved. She might believe otherwise, but their estrangement wasn't anything he'd planned.

Like their marriage, it just happened.

And Ara neither knew how to fix whatever had broken them—nor did he think it was worth fixing. Zaynab shouldn't have ever been with him, and since he couldn't undo time and make it so that she never had met him, he figured the least he could do now was hear her out. Because she hadn't flown thousands of miles from the UK to coastal Somaliland for Anisa's engagement party.

So he should have been prepared when after ushering her out of the house and into his car, she opened her purse, pulled out papers, thrust them at him and said, "I want a divorce."

That word again.

Ara lifted a heavy hand and thumbed the ignition button, the steady hum of the engine not enough to drown out the pressingly dull sound of his heart beating in his eardrums. A sudden heat wrapped its hot, clammy fist around him and held him in its thrall, squeezing at his airway and forcing him to breathe more carefully through his nose—lest Zaynab realize what was happening to him.

Besides, once he breathed enough times and calmed his body's instinctual reaction, their divorce wasn't truly shocking news. More unwelcome as it added another task to his overflowing work schedule.

Convincing himself it was the additional unwanted workload she'd now dropped in his lap that was causing his startling physical reaction, Ara sat back, grasped the wheel and drove them away from the house and any prying eyes that might see them together. More than not wanting attention drawn from Anisa and Nasser announcing their engagement to their friends and family, he quietly admitted that he wasn't ready for his divorce to be made public yet.

They didn't speak again during the drive to her hotel.

And then only when they entered her modest hotel room.

"How did you know where I was staying?" she blurted as soon as the door to her room closed behind him.

He arched a brow. "You messaged me the location."

"Right. I forgot that I did that..." Zaynab turned her back on him, but not before Ara caught her anxiously sinking her teeth into her bottom lip. She dropped her purse and the papers she'd been holding onto her bed—the ones he hadn't taken from her yet—and she walked over to slide open her balcony door and let in a cool breeze.

Stepping closer to her, he tasted the ocean in the fresh mid-October air as it fluttered through her hijab and flooded the room. She must have an even better view of the Indian Ocean and Batalaale Beach from her balcony than he did from his hilltop house. If nothing else calmed him, it was looking out over the white sands of the beach and the sparkling blue waters that had been his home all his life. He would've hoped that the vista offered her the same serenity, but judging by the way her shoulders practically touched her ears and her arms caged her middle, Ara didn't think Zaynab cared much for the view.

He couldn't blame her. They were, after all, about to end their marriage.

Curbing a sigh, he asked, "If you planned to meet here, why did you come to the house?"

"I didn't mean to do that either. I just… I didn't want to wait anymore." A stronger breeze whipped at her headscarf, the black chiffon wrapped tightly to her head, a reminder that she hadn't removed it. It was the first time she'd done that. When they'd lived together, just the two of them, Zaynab never wore her headscarf around him. As husband and wife, she hadn't had to be modest with him.

He supposed that too would change once the divorce was official.

It was an odd thing to fixate on given the heavy subject they had to face.

Zaynab turned from the open balcony and looked at him, concern creasing her brow and a frown curling across her pursed lips.

"I hadn't planned to come to the house," she said softly, her arms banding around her tighter, "and I certainly wouldn't have come had I known about Anisa's engagement."

Ara frowned. *Yes*, he thought guiltily, that was his fault. Though in his defense, they rarely spoke and he assumed a call from him wouldn't be welcomed by her.

"I would've called with the news, but I figured you might be busy."

By the way Zaynab worried her bottom lip, he knew what they were both thinking about. Or rather, *who*.

Her mother.

Part of the reason he hadn't disturbed her was for her mother's sake. It would've been unfair to distract Zaynab when her mother required her undivided attention, and understandably so. They hadn't spoken about it, and Ara had only heard the news from one of Zaynab's distant relatives, but he couldn't imagine what she'd been going through after learning of her mother's cancer diagnosis.

It was one thing to lose family—he knew that all too well, unfortunately. And yet another to watch them suffer and not be able to do anything to help.

"How is your mother?"

If he hadn't known what to look for he'd have missed the slightest tremble to her chin.

"She's fine," she replied. "In remission now, alhamdulillah."

"Alhamdulillah," he echoed, with a lot more relief than he'd expected to be feeling. He had first met her mother, Fadumo, at his and Zaynab's nikah. Being that her only child was getting married, Fadumo had flown to Berbera from London for the special occasion. Though she had been there to support her daughter, Zaynab's mother hadn't treated Ara with anything but maternal kindness, and in that way she'd reminded him of his own late mother… So, naturally, he was relieved to hear that her health hadn't only improved but been restored.

Ara didn't fault Zaynab for not telling him that her mother had been sick during their marital separation. Not when they both must have known that this day would come.

That their divorce was imminent.

The awkward silence that followed had him shifting his weight from foot to foot. And the restlessness was compounded when Zaynab glanced at the papers on the bed.

Seeing that he couldn't avoid it any longer, he picked them up, tension priming his muscles as he perused the small sheaf of papers. It didn't take him very long to relax. And then to grow confused.

"This is an application form for a khula." He directed his scowl from the papers to her stubborn expression.

She jerked her head in short affirmation, a look of determination staring back at him.

A khula was the only way a wife could initiate divorce proceedings.

"I went ahead and spoke to my local Muslim law council," Zaynab explained when he didn't speak. "We'd have to go through the application process, and I'd have to pay back your mahr—"

"No." The word slipped easily from his lips as he set the papers down on the bed. Fighting the urge to rip up the divorce application forms, he narrowed his eyes at her. "This isn't how we'll do this. Your dowry is not up for discussion." Although he knew without paying him back her bridal dowry, she wouldn't even be able to start the process of khula.

He would give her the divorce, but he'd do

it in a way where she wouldn't have to be deprived of the dowry he'd promised her.

"A khula is unacceptable."

"But I want this done now. I don't want to wait three months until it's official."

She was talking about iddah, the three-month waiting period. If *he* divorced her, Zaynab and he would still technically be married for three of her regular menstrual cycles. That meant she wouldn't be officially separated from him until after those three months.

"Did you intend to remarry?" He hadn't even considered that possibility, and he didn't care to, not when his thoughts veered toward a blistering anger and…jealousy. Denying it was pointless; he was jealous of what her impatience insinuated. Was there another man waiting in the wings, biding his time for Ara to be out of the picture fully? It would make sense why she seemed so disinclined to perform iddah. And it wouldn't shock him if there was a lover awaiting her eagerly.

Zaynab was a beautiful woman. It couldn't be hard for her to find someone to replace him.

"Is that why you're rushing to perform khula rather than a talaq?" The talaq was the more accepted practice of divorce, where the husband would initiate the divorce proceedings. It was far less complicated, and it wouldn't require her to return any part of her dowry. "I can't see why else you'd be impatient."

If looks could kill...

Well, he wouldn't be standing in front of her.

"After this I think I might not ever remarry," she said, seething, her words stabbing into him and fueling his bitterness more.

"Still, the iddah period serves a purpose," he argued.

"It's not even like pregnancy is an issue. Doing iddah would be a waste of time."

She had a point, of course. They hadn't ever consummated their marriage. And since the chance of immaculate conception was impossible, the three-month waiting period was unnecessary.

"That may be so, and yet I don't want to rob you of the dowry."

Zaynab rolled her eyes and kissed her teeth. "You wouldn't be robbing me—I'm *choosing* to give it back. Just sign your half of the papers…please, Ara."

His name came out as a softly exasperated plea, and it nearly weakened him into agreement.

"Pregnancy isn't the only reason the iddah exists," he heard himself say, his voice gruffer. "It's there as a measure to ensure a couple truly want a divorce, and that there's no path to a reconciliation." Sealing the distance between them, he stopped in front of her, the space between them vibrating with the heat of their bodies and the tension of their situation. "Divorce is hard enough without regrets."

Zaynab sniffed at his words. Being a few inches shorter than him, she lifted her chin to stare him down and it made him feel small.

Though not small enough to stop him from saying, "Are you so certain that we're beyond a possible reconciliation and any regrets?"

It was as though his brain and his mouth were disconnected. Ara couldn't explain why else he was pushing against the divorce so suddenly, especially since he wouldn't force Zaynab to remain with him. He told himself a year ago when she left him that it didn't matter what happened to their marriage and that it was for her to decide what she wanted. *That I would go along with whatever she desired.*

And she was clearly telling him that she wished for their relationship to end.

So why couldn't he just shut up, and do as she asked and sign the papers? It would be the rational course of action.

But apparently he was feeling irrational, because he cupped her cheek and stroked her soft skin, the simple touch unlocking an ancient primal part of him.

"Wh-what are you doing?" she stammered, her eyes widening but her body remaining still. She could've stopped him from touching her. Stepped back and ended the contact.

But when she didn't, Ara touched her a little more boldly. His hand slid down and framed her lower jaw, felt the tension buried beneath the smooth brown skin and deep in her jawbone. He tipped her chin back further, and with his thumb indenting the soft flesh of her bottom lip, Ara inhaled sharply when her mouth parted open, her tongue swiping out suddenly and wetting the tip of his digit. He could tell by the way her eyes widened that she hadn't meant to lick him. And yet that knowledge didn't douse the heat firing through his body.

They had come here to begin to finalize the end of their marriage.

And somehow he was now holding her, his arm secured around her back and their bodies pressed close. He turned them and walked her back toward the large, comfortable bed a few feet away.

Zaynab gasped when the back of her legs made contact with the bed and gave way, bending, bowing and sending her reeling backward onto the cushioned support of the bed comforter and mattress. Ara followed her, his hands pressed by the sides of her head, their chests no longer touching and yet both matched in their heaving breathlessness.

Her eyes rounded with shocked confusion, sparked with a newer emotion. Desire, he recognized quickly, feeling the same yearning pumping molten heat through his own body.

"I'm just making sure that we're both certain this is what we want." Ara took her chin in his hand again, his face lowering closer to hers until he could feel her sweet, warm breath stirring over his lips. "I can't walk away with any doubts. Can you?"

For a second she did nothing but swallow audibly, but then she shook her head, the motion causing her hijab to slide a little back off her forehead, the baby curls she'd smoothed at her hairline peeping out. Teasing him. Firing up his need to see more of her.

She didn't object or stop him as he revealed her. As he drew back the hijab with a gentle hand, she lifted her head to help him and he settled the material at the base of her neck, which only fueled the fire for his lust. He couldn't have worked fast enough, but the result was well worth his patient endurance.

"Braids," he breathed, pulling her hair free of the hijab that had restrained them and carding his fingers through the long, silky golden-brown lengths of her microbraids.

Ara lifted a palmful to his mouth, brushing their softness over his lips and groaning when he caught a tantalizingly sweet whiff of her hair. It wasn't enough for him to bury his nose into the hair he had trapped in his hand; he desired the source and moved to tunnel his face into the side of her neck, her braids tickling his face and the scent of her oud perfume, fruity shampoo and whatever was naturally *her*. Dazed by passion, he ended up with his lips pressed to the pulse beating right above her clavicle.

Her soft little gasp wasn't what drew his head up.

No, it was her hands at the back of his head, digging in suggestively until he rose up over her again, their lips in perfect alignment were he to descend to her.

Before Ara could decide whether he wanted to go as far as kiss her, Zaynab pulled him down to her and made the decision for him.

He groaned as her lips moved hesitantly against his, her soft exploration of him causing his arms to nearly buckle and testing the limits of his self-restraint to do anything more. But as he told himself that this was all it could be, he felt Zaynab's legs brushing his thighs, her ankles pressing into his backside with an urgency that matched the now-confident slide of her mouth against his.

It was counterproductive for them to be doing this—torturous even, considering why they had come together.

And as if to remind them again, the loud distinct crinkle of paper reached his ears.

She didn't break from his mouth, tipping her hip to the side while he ripped the offensive papers for the divorce application free from under her. Flinging them away haphazardly, not caring where they ended up or if they blasted to oblivion, he pushed her deeper into the bed and kissed her to breathlessness. And she returned the favor, driving him onto his back at one point and moving away from his mouth to nip and trail her lips along his jawline to a sensitive earlobe.

He knew he should've stopped them.

But it was when Zaynab lifted up the bottom of his shirt that Ara realized that even if he desired to, there was no ending what they had started, not without any hurt feelings. He hadn't been a good husband to her, but this one time he wished to give her what she wanted.

First this moment together, and then the divorce she asked of him.

CHAPTER TWO

ZAYNAB DIDN'T KNOW what made her angrier at Ara: that he'd abandoned her with a signed divorce application after their one-time passionate mistake, or that after refusing to give him any more thought, she was now fully reminded of him at her doctor's checkup.

She stared in horror as her family doctor confirmed what she'd suspected and dreaded.

"You're pregnant, Zaynab."

Pregnant? She was *pregnant*?

Whatever else her doctor said was slowly overtaken by her harsh, grating breaths as she barely held together her composure when all she wished to do was scream.

"Your HCG levels… It's a lot later in the first trimester…"

"I'm pregnant." She hoped that saying it would settle her thundering heart, but she only grew more faint sitting upright on the exam bed when her doctor smiled and nodded patiently. Zaynab didn't even bother asking her if she was certain. She had the result of her blood test in her hands, not to mention a pregnancy test currently occupying the dustbin in her flat's bathroom. She'd done the home screening when her usually regular cycle hadn't arrived not for one but two months. It hadn't taken her long to do the math after and then drop everything to visit the nearest chemist to her flat.

The home test had told her exactly what her doctor had: that in less than nine months she'd be a mother.

"It can be overwhelming even when it's anticipated, but especially when it's not. Know that there are options," her doctor told her with a meaningful look. "I have brochures explaining those details. I'll let reception know to pass them to you once we're done here."

Zaynab pressed her hand to her swooping belly and croaked, "Are we not done yet?" Because she'd heard plenty enough. Now all she wanted to do was leave the doctor's office, stop by the corner shop for ice cream and go home and pretend like none of this was happening. Like her life hadn't been irrevocably changed in what felt like a blink of an eye.

And all for what? One ignorantly blissful moment of pleasure, that was what. Had she known the bliss was a ticking time bomb, she might have reassessed allowing the reptilian portion of her brain to have its fun.

It physically pained her to listen to the doctor's next instructions, the sterility of the information feeling both unreal and upsettingly her new reality.

"Since you're nearly at twelve weeks, we can begin certain genetic and blood testing. I'd also like to book you for your first ultrasound scan, if that's all right with you?"

Zaynab bobbed her head weakly.

And that was how the rest of her doctor's appointment went, and she left the office with brochures burrowed discreetly in her purse along with the times and dates for the next string of appointments for her prenatal care. The sun beamed warmly overhead as she stepped out into the chilly January morning, the snowfall from last night already mostly melted off the footpath except where it clung stubbornly in brown-topped patches to the curb. She couldn't believe that a little over a week ago, she was ringing in the New Year with the resolution that this year she'd focus on self-discovery and reclaiming joy for herself.

Though she had avoided thinking about him, Ara had been half the reason she'd made the resolution. The other half was inspired by watching her mother battle her cancer diagnosis and come out the victor.

Pride for her mother shone through her as brightly as the afternoon sun washing down over the gray rows of buildings in this part of the city. She turned her face up to the warmth, saddened that it couldn't melt the solid fear sitting heavily in her stomach the way it had the snow.

She groaned, remembering that her next chat with her mother would be interesting now that she was expecting.

And she wasn't the only person Zaynab would have to tell.

Despite how he'd cowardly sneaked away on her after taking her to bed, Ara had the right to know he was going to be a father. As daunting as it would be to send him the news, she would have to brave through it because the alternative of not telling him wasn't an option. But it didn't mean that she had to do it immediately. She'd just found out and needed her own time to process and sort through her feelings before she added any of his emotions to the mix.

Later, she promised. When she had her head on straighter and the timing was right. And likely over a voice message because she couldn't handle seeing his handsome face while she delivered the bombshell of an announcement.

She was nearly halfway to the bus stop when

her phone thrummed several times in succession with incoming texts before her ringtone nagged at her. The impatient caller turned out to be her childhood friend Salma reminding her they had a standing lunch date.

"You forgot, didn't you?" Salma clucked loudly.

Zaynab had forgotten, but she had a good reason. And she must have been quiet enough that Salma sensed it and asked more soberly, "Are you all right, love?"

"No, I'm pregnant," she said, the sob choking out of her surprising her. Because as wildly upsetting to her world as the news of her pregnancy was, she hadn't once felt the urge to cry until then when a familiar voice asked after her well-being.

Salma comforted her over the phone until they met face-to-face, their lunch plans at their favorite restaurant canceled for takeout at Zaynab's flat on her well-worn but comfortable leather sofa and a sitcom playing on the TV. Much later when she'd calmed down, Zaynab followed Salma's gaze to the open and half-packed luggage in the corner of the sitting room.

"I almost forgot about that…" Zaynab trailed off with a sigh. In a few days she was due to leave for a work-related trip to Mauritius. She'd been looking forward to the trip until this morning when her world had been upended. But as much as she'd like to call in sick, her agency wouldn't be able to send a replacement so easily. Working as a personal support care worker was fulfilling, and her current position of two years was with a client she'd grown to care deeply for. Opaline was a sprightly octogenarian in spite of her knee replacement, double hip replacement and recent cataracts surgeries. It hadn't stopped the elderly woman from accepting an invitation to attend a family member's wedding in the beautiful East African islands.

She'd not only invited Zaynab, but Opaline had also seen to it that her grandnephew and attorney-in-fact, Remi, had paid for Zaynab's ticket and accommodations as well as her meals. Remi was counting on Zaynab to care for his great-aunt during their travels. Their generosity meant a lot to her, and it was why she wouldn't cancel on them.

"Come on. I'll help you pack," Salma said, her smile sympathetic. Being a nurse, her friend understood the grueling hours of the workload in their chosen fields.

It was hard carving out time for herself when it was in her nature to care for others.

Her mother when she'd been battling her cancer.

Opaline and Remi.

And now a child that would rely solely on her. She touched a trembling hand to her abdomen.

So much for my New Year's resolution...

Later when Salma had helped her finish packing and called it a night, Zaynab sat in her flat alone. She stared at the phone gripped in her hand and the message she had hastily thumbed out before her nerves got the better of her.

I'm pregnant, and it's yours.

The last part seemed redundant and it had churned her gut to even type it, but she didn't want him mistaking or doubting who was responsible. Not that she believed that Ara was the type to shirk his duties, and yet he hadn't been a real husband to her, or even much of a friend.

"You never really trusted me," she murmured.

But that wasn't her problem right now.

She hovered an aching thumb over her screen, rallying her courage to send the message before finally doing it. As soon as the text started a new chat with him, Zaynab shut her phone off and dropped it on the cushion beside her, knowing that whatever response it generated from him would be a worry for her tomorrow.

Ara hadn't worried much about how his tomorrows would look, mostly because he planned so far in advance that not much took him by surprise.

Not his sister Anisa's engagement announcement—he'd seen the attraction between her and Nasser long before they had acted on it. And not anything else related to his life, professionally or personally.

In fact, not since his parents' deaths had he felt the groundless sensation of true, utter shock.

But Zaynab's message was a close second.

I'm pregnant, and it's yours.

Those five words had circled his brain—taken over dominion of every thought, and stymied most of his action for days after Ara had received her news. His distraction was poorly timed as he'd traveled from home for important business. Business that required his full and undivided attention, not that he blamed Zaynab. It wasn't news that he would've wanted her to hide from him, even though she could have concealed her pregnancy and the truth of him being an expectant father.

With how Ara had treated her, he would have expected her to never contact him again.

Beyond feeling relieved that she hadn't hidden it from him, he couldn't specify exactly how he felt besides this hollowness. It wasn't all that helpful that he didn't have much time to himself to sift through his feelings about becoming a father.

Between back-to-back meetings, he barely found the time to sleep or sit for a meal.

But if his sleep deprivation and slight malnourishment was what it took to seal this latest business deal, then he would gladly suffer it.

As the owner of Africa's largest shipping company, Titancore Transport, his shoulders carried a tremendous weight of responsibility for the thousands employed by him and his clients, but now Ara was looking to do more for his country too.

A total of three days elapsed before he finally deigned that the business proceedings were going smoothly enough and could be handled by some of his trusted executive staff. No sooner had Ara made the declaration did he begin to board a privately chartered flight for Mauritius.

Although he'd been tied up, he had looked into Zaynab's whereabouts, not knowing if she was still in her London flat or residing with her mother in the English countryside.

It was surprising when he discovered that she was in far closer reach to him. In less than five hours his plane was touching down and taxiing toward the one passenger terminal at the Sir Seewoosagur Ramgoolam International Airport, Mauritius's primary airport.

He had a car awaiting him on arrival. By the time the car stopped in front of the resort's main entrance and he stepped out to be greeted by staff, he willed patience that he wasn't whole-heartedly feeling and sought details of Zaynab's room.

Ara clenched his jaw at the memory of fall-ing on Zaynab like an animal. It had been over two months ago since she'd come with her di-vorce application, but it might as well have been yesterday with how vivid the memories play-ing in his mind were. And with those memo-ries came the awakening of a familiar hunger to take her in his arms again and repeat what they'd done step by step, as though his slip in judgment hadn't caused the situation they were now in. Instead of entertaining his powerfully magnetic attraction to her, he should've been ashamed of his senseless and unalterable mis-take. Should have been preparing to grovel at Zaynab's feet for burdening her. But each step that carried him closer to her eroded his shame and, in its place, a heady anticipation to reunite with her arose.

An anticipation that hadn't existed a few days earlier. Before she'd messaged him with the an-nouncement of her pregnancy, he'd been certain she wouldn't contact him ever again once he had done as she desired and signed her divorce application. Their lives were different enough that they'd likely never cross paths, and if for some reason they did, Ara didn't torture himself into hoping that she'd speak to him. *That she'd forgive me.* After all, it would only be fair that she treated him with the same indifference he'd shown her in their short marriage.

At least that was what he envisioned would come next. Only now that had changed...

Because of their whirlwind passion, fate had forced them together.

In a matter of a briefly worded text he'd gone from expecting never to see her again to figuring out how to keep her in his life for as long as he breathed, and the absurdity of it had Ara indulging the smile lifting his mouth.

Slashing a hand down his face a moment later, he schooled his features into neutrality as he spied her suite up ahead, the number on the door like a beacon. But as eager as he'd been to be near her again, Ara found himself shifting on restless feet as reluctance gripped him in front of her door.

He couldn't be sure what lay on the other side, but he only hoped that she would hear him out once she opened the door.

With that he raised his hand to knock—

Only for the door to swing open, his fist breezing through midair before he drew his hand back, his scowl immediate.

The man blocking his path had at least a couple inches or three on Ara, and though his lanky limbs looked weaker in his well-tailored suit, he compensated with an unspoken air of authority that rivaled his own.

Authority that threaded his demanding tone when he asked, "Who are you?"

Before Ara could tell him that he'd taken those words right out of his mouth, a sweet voice Ara would have recognized anywhere called out, "Remi? You haven't left yet—"

Rounding the corner of the entrance hall, Zaynab cut herself off and stopped in her tracks as Ara's eyes locked on her.

He'd envisioned their reunion so many different ways over the course of the past few days, yet he hadn't considered the surge of emotions seeing her would unleash in him. Desire blended with satisfaction and intrigue as Ara trailed his gaze over her. Like this stranger she'd called Remi, she was dressed as though she were heading to an event. Threaded with a bevy of sequins, the pale gray floor-length maxi dress whispered over the polished white floor tiles as she walked a couple steps toward him, the surprise that had seized her beautiful round face framed by a white lightweight hijab.

"Ara?" she whispered his name in a way that shouldn't have stirred him below the belt but did. "What are you doing here?"

"You know him," this Remi asked her, ignoring Ara completely now and irritating him in doing so. But what annoyed him even more was Zaynab shifting her stare to Remi and nodding.

Jealousy surged through Ara and sat over his chest like a weight as she bit her lip and gave Remi an embarrassed smile. Whoever this man was to her, he clearly mattered enough to warrant not only her shy feelings, but an explanation.

"He's my—*was* my husband."

Her deliberate use of the past tense hadn't gone missed, and if he weren't in their company, Ara might have clutched the spot above his heart that panged the hardest at the blow of her words. Instead, he stared hard at her and said, "We need to talk."

Not that it mattered to Ara, but Remi's frown flicked between them. "Would you like me to stay?"

Ara had to check the urge to grab him by the collar, heave him out of the room and slam the door closed behind him. But he refused to devolve into a beast, even though an animalistic anger pulsed through him and tensed and primed every tendon and muscle in his body.

Zaynab calmed him a bit when she shook her head. "No, that's all right." Then with another of her smiles, she said, "I already held you from the party long enough. Please, tell Opaline that I'm fine and I just need a little rest."

Remi hesitated, but in the end he nodded curtly at her, leveled a glare on Ara that clearly was a parting warning and then stalked off in his highly polished leather shoes after Ara cleared out of his path.

Ara entered the resort suite and closed the door after him. As his hand released the door handle he suddenly had a flash from the past, when he'd done the same thing back in Berbera, and how their conversation in her hotel room had led to them sprawled in a sweaty tangle of limbs in her hotel bed.

Closing his eyes and balling his fists at his side, he took a moment to strengthen himself before he opened his eyes and turned to Zaynab.

She had moved back from him, her arms crossed and her wary look telling him everything she didn't need to. She was worried by his presence, and that was the last thing he wanted to make her, and not only because she was carrying his child.

It was as if everything clicked into place right then, seeing her, knowing that she was now bound to him in a way that was above law.

He hadn't known what to feel when she told him of her pregnancy, but now—*now* Ara reflected on how he'd nearly lost his life a year ago. How empty and purposeless he'd felt when he had first lost his parents sixteen years before that, how he had focused so hard to be all the family his sister needed, and how he'd poured his whole being into expanding on the business he had inherited from his mother and father. As accomplished as it might have looked on the outside, he could no longer ignore that it hadn't filled the ever-present, ever-hungering void deep within him.

But he had his answer finally, his eyes resting on her stomach.

Their child might not have been planned by either of them, but it was exactly the purpose Ara had been waiting for. And like every true purpose, a plan needed to follow. His idea was not only self-admittedly ludicrous; there was also the added pressure and extra hurdle of getting the child's mother on board.

And judging by the way Zaynab's eyes began to narrow in suspicion, Ara didn't believe for a second convincing her would be easy.

CHAPTER THREE

"YOU STILL HAVEN'T told me what you're doing here." Zaynab heard the nervousness trembling through her voice, despite having quietly and fervently hoped that she wouldn't sound as weak with shock as she felt in seeing Ara again. And of all the places she wouldn't have thought to ever see him.

Mauritius was supposed to be the place for her to reset her emotions and get a grip on her new and reeling reality of pregnancy. She knew that she would eventually have to speak to him, but she had chosen to ignore the text she'd sent him until she returned home. It would have given her the time to figure out how to handle his feelings about their new shared responsibility.

That's assuming he even wants to be in our child's life.

But now it was apparent that fate had another plan in store for her.

And there was no point in her hoping that he hadn't received her text and just shown up for some other unexplained reason. She curled her fingers under her elbows and wrapped her arms around herself tighter, feeling safer under the lasering power of his hard, assessing stare. The coldly blank set to his handsome face was typical for him. She could count on one hand how many times he'd smiled around her, and none of those few times had ever been directed at her. Sometimes she wondered if the issue of their marriage—the true reason why they couldn't make it last was because of her.

Was it that he didn't want to be with me?

They hadn't married for love, she had known and accepted that. And if it hadn't been for Sharmarke…

Zaynab didn't think of her father too often, and when she did, she never really thought of him as her *dad*. He hadn't been in her life past the first ten years, choosing his political career as a statesman over his family. Then her parents divorced and she moved from Somaliland to the UK with her mother. Now at thirty-seven, she hadn't cared to renew a relationship with him, but when he'd called her out of the blue a little more than a year ago, she hadn't been able to shut him out of her life. Mostly because her mother had been so thrilled that they were bonding. Zaynab would do anything to make her happy.

But if she were being honest with herself, she had also been curious to know more about her father. She'd spent the better part of her childhood and a bit of her adulthood starved of his attention and now, suddenly, not only had he popped up, he'd also shown *interest* in her.

At first Zaynab had maintained her firm and thorny defenses, keeping their discussions brief and only ever over texts. Slowly those texts became phone calls, then video chats before finally Sharmarke surprised her with a visit, and naturally she'd forgotten to keep her guard up and seemingly forgiven him of his past absenteeism. The hope she hadn't bothered with then made her *believe* that she could trust Sharmarke. Made her think that he wanted to be a proper parent to her.

That he loved her…

And pathetically she'd thrown open the doors to her heart and her life and let him in, never once imagining an ulterior motive.

For a while everything had been perfect. She had both her mum and dad in her world, and they felt like a real, normal, *happy* family doing real, normal, everyday things together. So normal and happy in fact that sometimes she wondered whether she'd dreamed up the whole thing. That in some delirious, desperate state that she had fantasized the perfect family scenario. And that any moment she would wake up and realize that none of it had been reality. Even then she'd known it had been too good to last.

So when Sharmarke had suddenly asked her to consider an arranged marriage that would be good for his business connections and revealed his true intentions for seeking her out and nurturing a relationship with her, she'd known her wake-up call had come. Zaynab keenly remembered alternating between wanting to burst into tears and screaming out her bitterness and devastation at him. In the end she'd been left chilled to the bone by her so-called father's cold betrayal. Spurred on by vengeance, she had agreed to meet this man Sharmarke was trying to get her married to. Then the plan had been for her to ruin the meeting, chase her would-be suitor away and embarrass her father before cutting off all contact with him for good.

But that hadn't happened, she thought sadly. Because despite being certain that any marriage Sharmarke had a hand in wasn't for her, she had fallen instantly and incomprehensibly in love with Ara the moment she laid eyes on him. The instant that his darkly magnetic stare locked its intensity on her and made her feel like no one else existed in his world.

She should be ashamed of herself but recalling that first meeting always put a silly smile on her face to her utter frustration.

Zaynab quietly sighed, looking warily at him as he closed the door and turned to face her. She flinched at the way his dark brows slashed over even darker eyes that narrowed as he walked forward and closed the short distance to her.

He stopped just as she began wondering and worrying if he meant to embrace her. It was fanciful thinking, of course, because aside from that one blip a couple months ago, Ara hadn't ever shown her physical interest. Most of their conversations had to do with impersonal subjects like their respective careers. They barely even spoke about their families; Ara seemed to avoid mentioning his sister and his late parents, which led Zaynab to believe there was not much point of speaking about her mother and her own childhood when it appeared he didn't care about her enough to ask or wonder.

Only now, in a twist of irony they were compelled to speak about family.

Their own. Because it was growing inside of her, and in a little over half a year, they would be parents.

Six months.

She wished he'd given her more time. Heck, it would've been nice if he'd let her know that he was going to drop in on her unceremoniously.

Which reminded her that he still hadn't answered her and explained why he'd shown up unannounced and how he'd known to look for her in Mauritius of all places.

Annoyed and curious now, she felt her brows puckering as she asked, "How did you know I was going to be here?"

"I have my methods," he said with a jerk of his chin over his shoulder. "Who was that man to you, and what was he doing in your room?"

Zaynab had a hard time picking her jaw up off the floor at his very plain insinuation and sheer audacity, otherwise she would have lashed him with her tongue sooner.

"Not that it's your business, but he's my employer, because I just happen to be working." She bristled, unfolding her arms and holding them stiffly at her sides despite wanting to throttle him. "And he was in my room because I wasn't feeling well and he walked me from the wedding party his family are all attending."

Ara's expression changed in a flash, his coldly impassive face flickering with concern. "What's wrong?"

Zaynab could hardly believe her eyes and

was stunned into silence. *He cares*... But then she watched his focus sail down to her stomach, and her heart sank, dropping down to the very spot where his eyes were trained. *The baby*, she mused. Of course it was their baby he was worried about, not her at all.

Biting back down her annoyance, she snapped, "I was a little queasy. Considering my current state, I've been told it's normal enough." She passed a hand over her lower stomach and watched in fascination as his own hands curled into fists at his side. Almost as though he wanted to touch the proof, feel the new tautness to her belly and set aside any doubts that he might still hold that they were expectant parents.

"How?" he rasped and caught her off guard when he flipped topics.

Zaynab arched a brow and sniped, "'How' what? How did I get pregnant? Or how does pregnancy occur?" Goading him was probably not her brightest idea, but he had asked the annoyingly obvious question, and in doing so made her feel somehow like it was her fault. Meanwhile in all likelihood he wasn't blaming her at all.

"You're upset," he observed silkily.

Clutching onto her anger and refusing to be weakened by the sound of his voice, she rolled her eyes at him. "I'm tired and my stomach still feels a little upset, so excuse me if I seem inhospitable right now." Then because she couldn't handle not squirming under his quiet assessment, she spun on her heels and padded barefoot back to where she'd been lounging on the patio. Ara followed her outdoors, his stare all that much more powerful when he was standing over her lounge chair.

Again, fighting the urge to wriggle like prey under his predatorial gaze, she waved to the chair beside her with a quiet invite.

He was here now. They might as well talk about their future, even if she was still getting used to the idea that Ara would now be in her life forever, although it wasn't in the way that she had once thought it would be. Their marriage might have ended, the paperwork filed and submitted and only waiting to be approved, but now they were going to be parents, whether they liked it or not. Or at least she would be because she hadn't considered any of the other viable options.

As shockingly unexpected and upsetting as it first was, over the past few days she knew in every fiber of her being that she wanted this child, just as deeply and madly as she'd wanted its father once.

Unlike Ara though, their baby would be a part of her life.

She wouldn't ever force him to be a father, knowing that he had to want to do it on his own and with no compulsion from her, no matter how much she would've liked for him to be in their baby's life. Besides, it wouldn't be the first man in her life who hadn't wanted Zaynab. For the better part of her existence, her own father hadn't wanted anything to do with her.

It was a truth that was still hard to swallow sometimes.

Although mostly her mother had been more than enough for her, it hadn't stopped Zaynab from picturing what her upbringing might have been like with Sharmarke around. Would they have had regular father-daughter outings? Would he have proudly placed her photo on his desk and humblebragged to his friends about her whenever he had the chance?

Zaynab would never know.

If she could prevent her child from feeling the same painful thoughts and doubting their self-worth, then she would try. But it would help if Ara made it easier to read him. As always, he made it hard to tell what he was feeling or thinking. And without some direction, Zaynab didn't know how to begin to untie her tangled thoughts.

"What do you want to do?" Much like his last question, he surprised her.

"Honestly, I haven't given it too much thought. I only found out recently. I'm still processing what it means for me now." Zaynab chewed the inside of her cheek before continuing, "All I know is that I want to keep the baby."

She wanted the baby. Ara's relief sagged him forward where he sat on the lounge chair across from her.

He hadn't even considered that she might not desire the pregnancy, but now that she'd said it, it eliminated a fear that hadn't had the time to fully manifest. Ticking that off the mental checklist he had running, he asked her, "What else?" However he could make this easier on Zaynab, he would. After all it wasn't him that had to do the heavy lifting, at least not initially. He wanted this to go as smoothly for her as possible.

"I want to remain in London," she said, her tone firming and letting him know that there was no further discussion to be had. "Also, a forewarning—once the baby's born, I might move to live with my mother initially. In case I need help for the first month or two."

Okay. That was something he *had* thought

of and was a huge part of the plan he began brewing quietly.

"I'm not going to force you to move to be in their life," Zaynab said this with a hand resting over her belly, "but it would be nice for you to be. That is, if you want to."

She sucked in her bottom lip and looked away from him making Ara understand that this was something she'd thought of, his possibly not wanting to be in their baby's life. Suddenly he had to wonder if she meant what she said. If she wasn't trying to push him away and hadn't made future plans of her own, that is. Plans that didn't include him being in the picture. On some buried rational level Ara knew that he shouldn't, but his mind veered back to the encounter with her employer, Remi, or whatever she'd called him. She had smiled familiarly at the man, and there was obviously some bond between them that had made Remi care for her.

Perhaps she had moved on.

Perhaps their relationship was more than boss and employee.

He wouldn't be shocked if it were true. Remi would be a fool if he couldn't see that Zaynab was a catch of a woman. Both beautiful and with brains that had drawn Ara to her in the first place. From their first meeting, he'd been taken with the way she handled topics from politics to sciences with an earnestness that had them talking for many hours. She had engaged his mind in a way no woman before her had.

And he was certain no woman after her would either.

Now that he'd lost his chance with her, fiery envy at the lucky man who would woo and win her over ate away at him.

Maybe that was why Ara tossed caution out and, rather than gently guide her toward the idea he'd had, he came right out and told her.

"We should move in together."

Zaynab goggled at him. "Move in together?" She repeated his words back barely above a whisper. She blinked owlishly, her hands then tensing over her stomach right before she shot up to a seat…and swayed in place, her eyes squeezing shut—

He reached forward, his hands securing around her shoulders while his heart seemed to have launched up into his throat. Breathing harshly, he looked her over, her closed eyes having snapped wide open as soon as he touched her. The last time he'd been that close to her it had led to them kissing and then creating the life that now grew in her.

"Are you all right?" He gritted his teeth, fear for her well-being still gripping him.

"It's just a little dizziness when I sat up too quickly."

She brushed his hands off her with a frown, not seeming to feel the same spark of heat he'd felt when they came into brief contact.

Her confusion having vanished quickly, she said, "Did you just propose that we move in together?"

"I did."

"Why?"

"I want us to properly raise our child."

He thought his response more than sufficient, yet Zaynab gawked at him. Speaking slowly and carefully enunciating every syllable as she might with a young child, she said, "And how does us moving in together have anything to do with that?" And then before he could answer, she raised a hand, palm up to show that she wasn't finished speaking.

"Actually, you don't need to answer that because my answer is no."

"No?"

"No," she stressed. "We don't need to raise our child under one roof. I'm happy that you would like to be in their life—thrilled to bits, really, *but* I don't see why we can't co-parent separately."

"It would be easier for one," he drawled, "less demanding for a child to be ferried between separate homes and less taxing on us."

Zaynab only huffed and turned her nose up at him, appearing nowhere close to warming to his proposition. "That's not a good enough reason to live together."

"Then we do it because we're married."

Now she eyed him like he'd grown an extra head right in front of her. "No-o-o," Zaynab stretched the syllable, "we aren't. I filed the paperwork already."

"That might be true, but if my calculation is correct, you haven't finished your iddah period."

"So? I know how iddah works. We'd have to be intimate for our divorce application to be null and void, and we haven't been since I filed."

"Again, you're correct. However your new… *condition* changes that." Ara looked pointedly at her stomach, an edge of possessiveness clanging in him every time her hands touched the area. He flexed his fingers open and closed as discreetly as possible, knowing that any contact with him would likely not be welcomed by her just then, not when her eyes narrowed in an accusatory glare.

"Explain," she demanded.

He obliged her. "Your pregnancy stretches the iddah period to until your due date."

"That's barbaric!" Her brown cheeks were

rosier, anger seeming to brand onto her glowing skin.

"Not barbaric, logical. It reduces the...*question* of parentage."

Fire and frost flashed in her eyes. "Is that what this is? Are you doubting me?"

"I'm not," he said quickly and sharply, his flared nostrils an indication that his temper was rising now too. But how could it not when she was being so difficult? He locked his jaw and calmed much of the gruffness from his tone before he replied, "I hold zero doubts that is my child in there. It's why I only want what's best."

Ara rose slowly, fighting against the instinct to stay by her side but knowing that she needed time to absorb what he'd told her. "Since I've said my part, I'll leave you to gather your thoughts and contact you later."

She glowered at him and pruned her lips in defiance, refusing to speak to him.

That was fine by him. There wasn't a point in forcing her to agree. Zaynab had to want to do this with him or it wouldn't work.

Though Zaynab was in Mauritius to work, it wasn't hard to enjoy the sunny island when her employers were determined that she not spend every moment working. Between a litany of pre- and post-wedding parties, Remi had lined up a list of activities for her to do with him and, if his great-aunt's health allowed her, Opaline occasionally joined them too.

Her guilt that she wasn't more grateful to Remi's thoughtfulness was only amplified when he took her on a picnic and hike, just the two of them, and he'd been careful to keep her on an easier trail. The picnic was delicious, the hike through the jungle trail thrilling, but it was the surprise of a scenic waterfall at the end that had her feeling rotten that she wasn't as present in mind as she would've liked to be. All Zaynab could think of was the inevitable answer she'd have to give to Ara soon.

The answer she was sure he'd come hunt for himself if she took too long.

But then Remi got a call that pulled him away, and since he couldn't take it right beside the roaring waterfall, he hurried back up the trail that had gotten them there, one ear pressed to his phone while he covered his hand with the other ear.

Zaynab watched him go before she sighed and faced the natural curtain of water and its shallow pool. She pulled her sneakers and socks off, suddenly wanting to feel the cool chill of the stiller pool, her skin itching from the rise of humidity. The rainfall from earlier only added to the cloying heat in the jungle's atmosphere and made her wish that she'd brought a swim-suit. Not that she'd have gone swimming with Remi watching.

Sighing again, she settled with gathering up her long skirt and treading through the water until she waded up to her knees. Then she tipped her head back and closed her eyes to the spray of water now sprinkling her face like the wings of a moth, an easy smile pulling at her lips.

If only she could remain this relaxed, maybe she could find the strength to face the so many unknown variables of her future.

Would she be a good mother? Could she be enough for her child if things didn't work with Ara? And now that she was thinking of him, why was he really pushing for them to move in together?

What's his agenda?

Zaynab didn't know how long she stood there, but her calves cramping was an indication. Just as she was in the middle of bidding the water-fall a quiet farewell, she heard a stone rustle and crack against another stone behind her on the embankment to the pool. Remi had to be back.

She glanced over her shoulder, the greeting on her tongue vanishing as she saw it wasn't Remi at all, but Ara.

Zaynab watched him silently as he left his

shoes by hers and treaded through the water to her. She waited until he was beside her to peer up at him. "Did you follow me here too?" she asked sullenly. "What happened to giving me time to think?"

"It's been nearly two days, and my patience has its limits."

"Well, I don't have an answer for you."

Rolling up the sleeves of his dress shirt, he stared back at her quietly. Meanwhile the powerful spray and misting waters around them steadily soaked his shirt into clinging to and shaping the thick, corded muscles typically hidden beneath his business suits. Muscles she'd gotten a feel of just once and admittedly still secretly lusted for.

Gulping now, Zaynab looked away from the temptation he posed her. "I wasn't living with you during most of my iddah, so why does it have to be different now?"

"That was my mistake. I shouldn't have let you go then."

"You walked away," she corrected bitterly, the sting of waking up to a bed all alone forever imprinted in her mind.

"I did, and I shouldn't have done that."

She wanted to ask why he had, but the truth frightened her, the possibility that maybe she wasn't enough for him or their marriage. And

Ara didn't offer an explanation, his low, gruff voice filling her ears as she turned her head off to the side where he wouldn't see how she furiously blinked back tears.

"Six months," he declared, piquing her interest. "If in that time we can't live together… peacefully, then we figure out how to co-parent separately."

"And our marriage?" she wondered. She wasn't rushing to hope that he would be reasonable, though if he really meant what he said, maybe they could figure this out together as a united front. Not married anymore, but happily raising their child.

"At the end of the six months, the end of your iddah, if you still wish for a divorce, I will give it to you."

His face was still unreadable, but she couldn't detect deception. Intuition told her that she could trust him to uphold his word.

As if reading her mind and sensing that she'd become more amenable to his outlandish suggestion to play house together, Ara shifted to face her and raised a hand between them, his thick brown fingers hovering, waiting— waiting on her permission to touch her stomach, she realized.

Nodding quietly, she clamped her teeth into

CHAPTER FOUR

SIX MONTHS!

Zaynab could still hardly believe that she'd agreed to living with Ara for six *long* months, or roughly what remained of her pregnancy. After she had been so adamant that his suggestion was an awful idea, and she was certain she wouldn't ever agree to it, it hadn't taken long for her to fold.

She blamed the beautiful waterfall and her softness for him.

If she closed her eyes, Zaynab could see Ara staring at her heatedly, his shirt soaking wet from the misty spray of the fall's gushing waters, and his hand warming her fluttering stomach—

She shook her head, annoyed by the blush now heating her face. If it had been his strategy to obliterate her resolve with desire, then he'd succeeded. Of course it only highlighted why she shouldn't have agreed. Why this idea her bottom lip and held still as he slowly reached for her.

She freed the breath she'd been holding when his warm palm skated over her belly lightly before settling with his fingers outstretched. Zaynab looked down where he held her and then slowly drew her eyes up to him, finding that he was far closer, his face much nearer than it had been. If she didn't know that all he'd wanted to do was connect with their baby, she would've believed he wanted to kiss her.

"Six months?" Ara asked her again.

"Six months," she heard herself agreeing.

of his posed a big problem. *I'm still weak for him.* Still hopelessly crushing on a man who hadn't taken their marital vows seriously and had pushed her from his life. Once she knew that he didn't love her, she had to escape. And she almost had until…

She crossed her arms to cover her belly and the baby they'd created together.

Despite her reservations—and the fact she was certain that this plan of his was still very much doomed—Zaynab grudgingly accepted that her pregnancy changed everything. It was why she was sitting beside Ara in his fancy white Porsche, speeding down a southbound motorway that cut through the sprawling metropolis of Mauritius's capital, Port Louis. If they were doing this, they'd have to talk seriously, and Zaynab knew they had to do it before she boarded her flight out of Mauritius that evening. So, as soon as she woke that morning, and with that clock ticking ominously in her head, she messaged Ara and asked to meet up after breakfast.

She anticipated that the conversation would be difficult.

What she hadn't expected was for him to propose they take a drive and have their serious discussion away from their luxury resort. She didn't think he had a specific destination in mind, but was a little curious when they seemed to be headed away from the northern part of the island.

Not curious enough to allow it to distract her, however.

"We should still divorce," she said, turning her head away from her passenger window and the panoramic sights of Port Louis.

Ara's side profile was hard to read even with her being close enough to breathe in the heady, knee-weakening scent of his fresh, citrus-bright cologne. She stiffened against the instinct to lean over the center console and sniff him. Sniffing him would send the wrong message, especially given she'd just told him that her mind wasn't changed where their divorce was concerned. Besides, mixed signals were the kind of thing that would complicate their already overcomplicated situation.

"Did you hear me?"

"I heard you," he said, his gaze briefly flickering off the road to her.

"Just because I agreed to live with you again doesn't mean our separation shouldn't still happen."

"If that's what you wish," was his rumbling response, as unemotional as his expression.

Zaynab stuffed down her rising frustration. Ara was telling her exactly what she wanted to hear, and yet his easy agreement chafed her and she couldn't quite place her finger on why it bothered her. And not wanting to really analyze what she was feeling in depth, she continued on as if she weren't perturbed.

"I'm still not convinced that moving in together is a good idea." Pressing her hands to her still-flat stomach, she said, "I want what's best for the baby."

"Then wouldn't that be having us both in their life?"

"That would be nice," she conceded. In a perfect world, she and Ara would be able to coparent while cohabiting in peace. No hormones driving her wild, tempting her every time those dark eyes of his zeroed in on her and made her want to silence any warning bells going off in her head and indulge every passionate thought Ara inspired in her…

And no heartbreak.

Because that was what she risked most if she was to live with him again. The first two months of their marriage had taught her not to entrust Ara with her heart. Instead of receiving the same love and attention that she was giving him, she'd ended up lonely and starved of the affection Ara should have given her. Surviving that isolation once took most of her will-power; doing it again might destroy any shred of strength she had left.

Zaynab's bottom lip trembled, and she blinked away the watery heat from her eyes and looked back out the car window and the passing cityscape. Breathtaking as Port Louis was with its position being picturesquely sheltered between the semicircle of verdant Moka mountains and the dark aquamarine waters of the Indian Ocean, she struggled to admire its beauty.

Silence reigned in the car, and it only made the noise in her head that much jarringly louder. Doubts clamoring to be heard one over the other.

What if he hurts me again? Can I trust him? Do I want to trust him?

Zaynab didn't have the answers. She only hoped she wasn't making a mistake by allowing Ara into her life once again.

Ara was no stranger to tense situations.

He'd dealt with them a number of times in his boardroom during tough meetings, and certainly whenever he angered his little sister, Anisa—which these days with her being stressed about her wedding plans was more often than not.

Yet all of his past experience abandoned him right then with Zaynab.

The awkward silence that started once they left the city limits of Port Louis lasted the hour-long drive from one end of the island of Mauritius to the other. Ara struggled to figure out how to break it. Every time he rustled up a bit of courage, he'd cast a quick glance at Zaynab and lose his grip on his bravery. Unlike him she didn't seem pressed by the quiet or look to be in a hurry to end it as she stared at her phone.

And why would she?

She'd restated that she wished for the divorce, making it clear that her agreement to live with him again had no bearing on their relationship…or the absence of it in this case.

Ara tightened his hands on the steering wheel, wringing the smooth leather until his fingers ached and the threat of callouses on his palms compelled him to ease his grip. It was one way to relieve the frustration choking him. Frustration born from the fact that he had only himself to blame for the tension between him and Zaynab. He hadn't been a good husband to her, and it had pushed her into leaving him.

And then he'd slept with her, not once considering their impassioned union would result in a consequence.

He couldn't change what had transpired in

the past, but he could do something about their future together. At least so long as he didn't give Zaynab a reason to change her mind. That was why the silence in the car was worrying.

Hearing their GPS indicate they were closing in on their destination gave him some hope though.

A large colorful billboard advertising the tea estate up ahead was the first break in the stretch of green pastures that ran alongside the main road. Zaynab lifted her head up, her focus no longer fixed to her phone screen.

"'The Bois Cheri tea factory,'" she said, reading the sign. "Is that where we're headed?"

"It is." He tried not to preen when Zaynab's breath hitched a few minutes later, the gush of rain-scented air that blew in when she rolled down the window prompting him to look her direction.

Ara hid a smile when she closed the window and gasped, "Oh, wow, it's beautiful."

A sight to behold, the neat green rows of tea plants climbed the hill and seemed to point to the expansive structure at the hilltop. As he turned the Porsche off the main thoroughfare and down a smaller lane that led to the structure, Ara had more trouble concealing his amusement. His lips twitched when a smiling Zaynab barely waited for him to find a spot

to park in the crowded lot outside the colonial
building before she unbuckled her seatbelt and
opened the car door. Meeting her outside, he
resisted puffing up his chest and led her to the
entrance.

There a staff member connected them with
their prepaid tour of the tea factory housed
within the estate.

As fascinated as Ara was to hear the long
history of the grounds and building and the
delicate, multistep process of tea cultivation,
in truth he was more invested in Zaynab's reaction to it all. She smiled politely as their tour
guide explained how the colonial rule of Brit-
ish, French and Dutch settlers had intermin-
gled with the local Mauritian culture, and she
beamed when they watched a demonstration of
the factory workers sorting tea leaves and bag-
ging them. Later, when they had taken a short
break during their tour, Zaynab easily struck
up conversations with some of the other tour-
ists in their group.

He'd forgotten how friendly she could be.

When their tour guide finally announced the
end of their walkabout of the estate building
and its grounds and encouraged them to explore on their own, Zaynab ventured toward
a footpath that led straight through the rows
of tea plants and the lake beyond. She stopped

and laughed a magical sound as a small curious boar strayed onto their footpath, blocking them from exploring the row of tea plants and the lake beyond.

Ara stepped in front of her instinctively the instant the wild pig snuffled closer, its snout raised up and its black eyes locking on Zaynab.

"It's not going to hurt us. It's just a piglet. Poor thing, probably lost its mother." Zaynab tutted at Ara and pushed past his defenses, her hand outstretched palm first as she cooed at the snuffling creature. Emboldened by her stillness, the small wild pig snorted softly and approached her. After a thorough sniff of her hand, she was given the green light to stroke its head.

"Did you lose your mother?" she asked, her voice soft and sweet.

Though every nerve in his body wanted to put himself between her and any source of danger, Ara clenched his jaw and forced himself to stand back. After all, it was only a tiny little pig. *What harm could it do her?* And he was rewarded for his patience when Zaynab let out a peal of giggles. The piglet ran circles around her, seemingly chasing its own tail. At the delightful sound of her laughter, a pleasant shiver chased down his spine and loosened the tension wringing his muscles.

But his momentary peace didn't last long. A sharp squeal nearby ended it quickly.

The wild boar that tore around the corner skidded to a halt, zeroed in on the piglet wriggling its small body and gave another angry squeal before charging straight for them.

Adrenaline slammed into him and erased the smile that had begun to pull at his lips. Not thinking of anything but needing to protect Zaynab, Ara's arm shot out and wrapped around her waist, pulling her toward him and away from the piglet. In one fluid move, he tucked her behind him and shielded her from the oncoming danger.

By that point the larger boar had slowed its charge, bristled in place and squealed sharply at them.

The piglet responded with a shorter, weaker squeal.

Ara held his ground, knowing that turning his back could open both himself and Zaynab to an attack from the unpredictable animal. Refusing to take his eyes off the angry boar that could only be the piglet's missing mother, he slowly and gently walked himself and Zaynab backward. The staring match ended when the piglet shot toward its furious parent. Giving them one last sharp-eyed look, the mother boar snorted and herded its youngling away.

Even after they were clear of the threat, Ara didn't budge until he registered Zaynab pulling free from him.

Standing beside him now, she laughed nervously. "Whew, that was a scary close call."

Scary didn't encompass the riot of emotion squeezing off his airways. He turned to face her, his hands locking around her elbows, eyes skimming over her. "Are you all right?"

"I'm fine," she reassured him.

Her words spoken gently weren't enough to convince him not to assess her for any injury. And he was silently grateful that she allowed him to do so. Once satisfied that she hadn't gotten hurt, Ara pried open his tightly clenched jaws and said, "The tea tasting should be beginning."

It was the perfect excuse to whisk her away back to the safety of the tea factory.

Again, he was thankful that Zaynab didn't struggle against him. Ara wished that was all it took to ease the disquiet fisting his heart. Like his mood, the clouds grew stormier, the pale gray churning darker.

They climbed to the second-floor covered balcony of the building where the restaurant operated when the rain started. Their small table, like the other tables all aligned in a row against the wooden railing, was set up for their private tea-tasting experience. Normally the stream of hot water from the teapot and the inviting steam curling up from his cup would have calmed him. Embedded in Somali culture, tea was a large part of his upbringing, and he'd always preferred it to a cup of coffee. Though right then he didn't think he could sample the assortment of herbal and black teas past the calcifying bile obstructing his throat.

He couldn't stop replaying the incident with the wild pig defending her piglet and how close Zaynab had been to bodily harm. And not just Zaynab, but their baby—

It would've been my fault. Because it had been *his* idea to bring her here.

Zaynab hadn't even seemed to care that she was nearly mowed over by an enraged boar.

"Are you okay?" Frowning at him, she lowered her teacup.

Ara forced his leg still and scowled, grumbling, "I'm fine."

"Really? Because you look ready to leap out of your skin," she remarked with raised brows. "Is this about the wild pig?"

She spoke as if the boar hadn't represented everything he feared happening to her without his protection. All he wanted to do was safeguard her and their child, and Zaynab wasn't helping him do that.

Why was she making this so difficult for him? And why was she fighting against their living together when it made the most sense to both be there for their baby?

Ara bit back his boiling frustration, knowing that unleashing it would have the opposite effect on Zaynab.

So, he attempted a different tactic. One he'd considered but had hoped he wouldn't need to use. Even thinking about his parents pained him as freshly as if they passed yesterday and not more than sixteen years ago. But it felt like a last resort now to get Zaynab on board with his plan.

"It is and isn't about the boar," Ara replied gruffly.

Blowing a sharp breath out his nose then, he continued, "Losing my parents changed my life. I wouldn't wish that loss on my worst enemy, and it's why I'm trying to do everything I can to keep our child from…from experiencing that too."

He hadn't been able to save his hooyo and aabo—hadn't even gotten to say goodbye and it haunted him still. If he could trade all his wealth to guarantee their baby never had to feel the pain he'd been dealt, he would do it in a heartbeat. But he didn't have that power alone. Zaynab had to want the same thing too.

"That's why I want us to be on the same page. It's why I think we should live together."

Zaynab looked down into her teacup, her fingertip circling the rim slowly. Waiting for her to speak her thoughts was torturous, but eventually she said, "I still don't think it's a good idea."

"Tell me why."

She sighed and met his stare. "I understand where you're coming from, and I want the same thing, but…"

"But…" he urged.

"*But* we've tried this already." Zaynab looked away, though not before he spied the pained expression flickering over her pretty face. "And we failed at that, didn't we? I might not know what it's like to lose a loved one, but my parents' divorce was ugly, and I—well, I just don't want that for our child either."

"I didn't ask for the divorce."

She whipped her head back to him with a ready glare. "I might have asked for the divorce, but that's only because it felt like the only solution. And I'd rather a clean break than be reminded that my marriage is a product of my father not truly wanting me."

They rarely spoke about Sharmarke. Zaynab's father was a barrier between them even though he was no longer in their lives.

"If what happened with your father is something you can't overlook—"

"What happened with Sharmarke has nothing to do with us," she cut in. Then, her eyes softening, she sighed. "I can't speak for you, but our marriage wasn't happy for me. And regardless of what my father did or didn't do, things would have ended up the way they did for us anyway."

Hearing that their divorce would've been inevitable for her stabbed into his chest. Worse, he couldn't do anything to assuage the pain as Zaynab was watching him carefully, her teeth locking onto and worrying her bottom lip.

"It's all right if you lay the fault at my feet."

"Why would I blame you for something *he* did?" she asked skeptically.

"Because I helped send him to prison."

It wasn't a secret that Ara had gathered the evidence against her father that had locked him away forever.

One of the hardest choices he'd had to make, but Sharmarke had allowed his political clout to get to his head and committed unspeakable, evil crimes against innocent people. It had fallen on Ara to either be his accomplice or to stand up against the injustice. He'd chosen the latter, and though he knew it had been the right decision—the morally good one, it hadn't made living with it any easier.

"It would be perfectly understandable if you blamed me."

"But I don't," she said firmly. "Sharmarke deserved the several life sentences for his crimes. If I'd known what he was doing, I would've locked him up myself. I should thank you."

"Thank me?"

She jerked her head in a nod. "I'm glad someone saw through his lies. Saw him for who he truly was."

Ara gazed at her in wonder, shocked to see no condemnation staring back at him. *She's not angry with me.* He had always thought that she secretly accused him of imprisoning her father. It was why he avoided the subject around her, and partly why he had spent their marriage avoiding her. At first he had wanted to protect her from who her father was, but after witnessing the harm Sharmarke had caused, Ara worried whether loving her would only bring him pain.

The kind of pain he'd felt after losing his parents.

They lapsed into their own little worlds after that, drinking their tea in a silence that was thicker than the misting rain falling outside.

"You know, six months isn't that long," Zaynab said, breaking the silence.

Then she smiled prettily and the sight of it delivered a bolt of crackling heat through him.

Ara wanted to agree, but with the way his heart was juddering, six months was already feeling like it would be a lot longer than he bargained for. He was doing this to protect her and their child, but now he had to wonder who would protect *him* from the heart-racing, chest-tightening, flushed skin feelings that Zaynab awoke in him every time he was close to her.

Feelings he highly suspected would only grow stronger if they moved in together.

CHAPTER FIVE

"DON'T FALL IN LOVE."

Sitting cross-legged on her sofa in her cozy little London flat, Zaynab lifted the pen off her small notebook and read over what she wrote.

It was the only rule she made for herself.

The only one that could wreck everything before it even started.

If she and Ara were going to make living together work, this one rule needed to be observed strictly. Because the last thing she needed was to forget that they weren't playing at pretend house, but rather trialing a co-parental existence that would provide the best environment for their baby.

Although Zaynab still thought living with him was a bad decision, she at least now understood why he was pushing for it so hard.

"Losing my parents changed my life."

Not once had Ara ever been that open about his feelings and thoughts. He could discuss business practices, politics and social ideologies all day, and that had attracted her when they had first dated, but she had imagined he would grow more comfortable around her after they married. She never knew what he was thinking and it made living with him difficult.

Yet for the first time ever, glimpsing his emotions had given her a wealth of information. One, he wasn't as coldly unemotional as she thought, and two, under his seemingly impenetrable exterior there was a beating heart that mourned his late parents.

"It's why I'm trying to do everything I can to keep our child from experiencing that too."

He'd spoken those words painfully and, now as they played back in her head, her chest tightened with her sorrow for him.

She could appreciate why family was important to him, and why he would want to be close to their baby, yet it didn't make moving in together any less nerve-racking. They had tried this before. It hadn't worked out for them then, and expecting a baby only exacerbated her apprehension. What if they argued? What if living with him stressed out her and the baby?

What if this is a mistake?

Either way Zaynab wouldn't know what it would be like until he finally arrived in London.

Their time in Mauritius was two weeks ago.

Two weeks since she last saw him, but Ara had begun messaging her regularly. He'd even sometimes call, and though never longer than a few minutes, she liked that he asked after her and the baby's health. It felt like they had talked more in those couple weeks than they had in all of their marriage. The promising change in him almost had her anticipating seeing him again.

Almost.

Seeing him meant having those dark eyes of his piercing her, his smoky, spiced cologne swimming through her space, and all the memories of his arms around her. And Zaynab just didn't know whether she was ready for that yet. "Or if I'll ever be ready for it," she whispered.

The doorbell ringing interrupted her musing.

In her hurry to answer her caller, she stubbed her toe on the small boxes she had piled right by the sofa. She had started packing slowly and hoped that she would be prepared when Ara arrived. With her apartment being so small, they'd decided that it was better to find a new place.

"Coming!" she called when the doorbell buzzed a second time.

She tugged down on the hem of her oversized hoodie over her leggings. Figuring it could just be a neighbor asking her for a cup of sugar, Zaynab went to the door.

A peek through the peephole told her it was not a neighbor calling.

Breathless, she opened the door with a shaky hand and faced Ara.

"Zaynab," he greeted. No "hello" or "how are you," just her name rumbled in that deep, deliciously sultry voice. She clamped down the urge to shiver in response, her clammy hand tightening on the door handle and pulling the door open wider.

In the short time apart, Ara hadn't changed except for one way: his beard was thicker and darker, and it only drew her eyes to his blade-sharp nose, sculpted cheekbones and dusky brown lips. His long overcoat was drawn open allowing her to a good look at the finely tailored three-piece suit he had on.

Somewhere out there she just knew some magazine was missing its cover model.

"May I?" he asked, pointing past her with the handle of his umbrella.

She blushed at having been caught ogling him, stepping aside and turning to watch him enter her home. Closing the door and sealing out the wintry air creeping in from the outside, Ara turned his back to her temporarily, leaving his umbrella against the door and his shiny leather shoes on the mat before facing her.

It gave her just enough time to get a grip

on her swooning when his familiar fragrance wafted over to her.

"Tea?" she offered with a meek smile.

He nodded and she flitted away into the open kitchen plan.

Feeling him shadow her, she busied herself gathering the teacups while the kettle warmed to a slow boil on the stove. She'd always thought her kitchen as a restful place, but that was before she had six feet of lean muscle looming behind her, reaching up over her head to help her pull down plates from the cupboards for the biscuits she'd planned to set up as a quick snack. It didn't matter that she could have reached for the plates perfectly fine herself. Her foolish heart thumped harder.

"The ultrasound."

Ara moved away from her to the fridge and plucked off the magnets holding their baby's first ultrasound.

It had been a few days ago since Zaynab had gone in for her scan. Ara had joined her over a video call, and although she'd appreciated that he had made some effort to be there for that special moment, she would have liked for him to have been there in person instead. Holding her hand when the sonographer had talked her through the process. Marveling with her as their baby made their first appearance on the technician's computer screen, the soft lub-dub of the heart filling the sterile exam room. And hugging her when she'd sat up and held the first ultrasound in her hands.

But she didn't want them to argue about it, not now that they were trying to be on the same page. So, she swallowed her disappointment.

"I have your copy of Button in my wallet. Remind me to give it to you later, all right?"

"Button?" he echoed.

Zaynab smiled, abashed that she'd have to explain. "Yeah, um, well it kind of looks like they've got a button nose."

Wrinkling his brow, Ara held the ultrasound at different angles. Zaynab could see him struggling to envision what she meant, and before she realized it, she was at his side, leaning in and pointing it out for him.

"Right there. It's just like a button, don't you think? Well, that and we can't keep calling him or her 'the baby.'"

"I see what you mean," he said, his warm, mint-scented breath stirring over her face as he turned his head to her. She'd been in such a rush to explain their baby's nickname that Zaynab hadn't considered personal boundaries. Now having infiltrated his space, she was even more susceptible to his magnetic aura.

With one look he made her feel like the only person in the world.

The only person in his *world.*

She gulped, her face heating up under his scrutiny, and needing his attention off her again, she nervously gestured to the grayscale image. "See, those are the arms, the little face, and the legs flung up over their head, like Button's doing yoga in there." She was babbling now, and Ara had to have known. Everything she was telling him he'd already seen for himself when he had joined her virtually for the ultrasound.

Worried about what she'd say next, Zaynab closed her mouth and retreated back to unpacking biscuits for them.

"When did you arrive?" she asked, using the excuse of plating their store-bought crisp biscuits to keep her back to him.

"Around noon."

Zaynab was glad she wasn't looking at him, otherwise he would've clocked her shock. It was past four now, so he'd been in the city for hours and he hadn't bothered calling her. Her confusion and irritation didn't last for long though as Ara explained himself.

"I would have come earlier, but I had an errand to oversee," he said.

"Errand? I didn't think you were familiar

with London." She knew that though Ara's company was big, and he had investors and clients all throughout the world, he preferred staying near his home in Berbera.

It was why Zaynab had worried he would change his mind about living in London and try to talk her into moving back to Somalia.

But seeing him now, in her tiny kitchen, allayed that fear.

At least it did until he said, "I had to see a woman about something."

"A woman? What woman?" She hadn't meant to blurt out her curiosity, or to whirl around to him and gawk, but the thought that he hadn't contacted her because he'd first gone to see another woman hurt more than she was expecting. Not that she was expecting him to be seeing other women. *And not that I should care...*

Ara's easy, handsome smile disarmed her suspicion though. "The estate agent," he said. "We need a home, don't we?"

Getting Zaynab out of her flat wasn't as difficult as Ara imagined it would be. As soon as he'd told her about the home he purchased, she was eager to see the place for herself.

Well, "eager" was a stretch.

Nervous was probably a better description. Throughout the hour-long drive from her neigh-

borhood to West London she gripped onto the
worn brown leather handle of her purse and sat
silently beside him. He'd been ready for her to
pelt questions at him, but he knew that she was
more likely still processing his sudden appearance at her doorstep. The only reason he hadn't
called beforehand and forewarned her of his arrival was because he'd wanted to see their new
home first and ensure that the estate agent he
had hired had done their job properly. It had to
be perfect for Zaynab...

Perfect for their growing family.

Family. That word was sitting better in his
mind with each passing day. Whether they divorced or not, they would be a family now, and
if Ara couldn't have Zaynab as his wife, then he
still wanted to provide for her and their baby.
As long as he breathed, they wouldn't go without anything. He silently swore the oath again,
as he'd done almost every day since he had last
seen Zaynab.

Now that he was with her, he was just ready
for them to truly begin this journey together as
soon-to-be parents.

And it started with showing her their home.

Zaynab's breath hitched, the brisk but soft
sound clapping like thunder in the silence of
the car. He glanced at her and fought a smile
when he glimpsed her wide-eyed awe.

After gearing the car into Park, he exited and circled around to grab her door before she did. She was still gawking out the windshield and whipped her head to him when he opened the door.

"This is it?" she squeaked the words out, stepping out of the car and straightening her baggy hoodie. In a hurry to see the new home, she hadn't changed out of her adorable outfit.

"This is it," Ara repeated.

Besides wrapping up his business affairs in Mogadishu, he'd spent the past couple weeks apart from Zaynab searching tirelessly for a home that would suit her. The staff at the estate company that he'd worked with had just about nearly reached their wits' ends when Ara had finally seen it; the ideal house for Zaynab. Ironically it was the antithesis of what he'd have chosen for himself. But one look at the pastel-hued stucco exteriors of the terraced houses in Notting Hill, the lush, private communal gardens, and tranquil atmosphere away from the busier central heart of London, and he knew he'd found the perfect home that complemented both him and Zaynab.

She pressed her hands to her stomach and softly wondered, "Which one?"

He opened a charming wrought iron fence, walked her beneath a dormant flowering tree covering their front property, and up a short flight of stone steps to their terraced house with a seafoam green door. Ara unlocked it and swung it wide open, gesturing for her to enter before him. He'd gotten a thorough tour from the estate agent and inspected every inch of the four-thousand-square-foot, three-story town house, which would now work to his advantage because he'd have nothing to disturb him from watching Zaynab's every single reaction.

Of course he wouldn't be able to do that if Zaynab remained rooted in the entrance hall, her lightly glossed mouth parted open and her head swiveling as she assessed her surroundings.

"Would you like me to give you a tour?"

She nodded slowly, closing her mouth but mesmerizing him with those large bewildered eyes of hers.

He couldn't blame her for being overwhelmed. The town house dripped with the kind of excessive wealth that surprised even him. Although with its hefty price tag, he expected nothing less.

Ara followed her facial cues as he guided her along the three separate flats that made up the grand town house. From the foyer to the sitting room, through the kitchen and dining area, and

into each of the six bedrooms and five bath-
rooms plus the cloakroom on the ground floor,
he highlighted the prime features of the home
that was theirs—but only if she wanted it to be.
And it was hard to tell what she was thinking
when her features remained fixed in surprise.

Nothing changed that until they came to the
end of the tour.

Then Zaynab asked, "Isn't it a bit...overly
done?"

Ara swept his gaze over the glamorous town-
home's primary bedroom, but unable to pin-
point what the trouble was, he shrugged. "Feel
free to redesign the decor to your tastes."

"It's not about taste," Zaynab stressed and
threw open her arms. "It's far too much space,
isn't it? It'll only be the two of us until I give
birth, and even then all of this is excessive.
Three families could live here."

"We're not letting any of the floors." Though
they technically could and keep one of the separate flats for themselves, Ara scowled at the
idea of having strangers in close proximity.
No amount of background checks would offer
him the peace of mind to allow that to happen.
He'd always known that people were unreli-
able. Zaynab's father came to mind. Sharmarke
had been like a mentor to Ara, tutoring him
in his university-level business courses, and

when his parents died, he'd become a surrogate father figure.

That was why it had felt like a betrayal to learn of the atrocities that Sharmarke had committed. Knowing that he'd willingly allowed that evil into his life was a reminder that Ara couldn't ever be too careful around others.

Even Zaynab could hurt him if he wasn't careful, if he allowed himself to give in to the fanciful thinking that this was about saving their marriage rather than providing the best life for their child. And in order to do that, Ara needed Zaynab to be content.

"If this house doesn't suit you, we can look at other available properties together," he suggested, frowning when she shook her head.

"No, it's not that. I just… I'm overwhelmed."

"So, the house is all right."

"It's perfect," she said with a snort and a roll of her eyes. "Are you kidding me? My mum wouldn't believe it if I showed her."

"We can have a guest room reserved especially for her for when she visits."

Naturally he would've thought Zaynab would be pleased by his suggestion, but her expression grew panicked.

Before he could wonder if he'd misspoken, she paced in front of him and said, "I haven't told you yet, but my mum, well she doesn't know that we're doing *this thing* that we're doing."

"Living together," he clarified.

"Yes, that. She doesn't know, and I'm not ready to tell her, so…"

"And you wish for me not to tell her either." Ara filled in what she was obviously struggling to ask of him.

"Please," she said with a nod, her hopeful little smile and beautiful brown eyes melting some of the ice that had seeped into him when he realized that he'd become some sort of dirty secret to her. Though nowhere nearly enough to keep him from clenching his jaw and jerking his chin in affirmation.

But he couldn't entirely let it go.

"Why hide it?" he asked.

Zaynab's smile slipped and she stopped pacing, looking away from him at the doors leading out from the bedroom to the balcony. "My mum doesn't know about the divorce. And I'm not ready to tell her about that either, especially now that it isn't final. At least not yet."

It wasn't the first time Ara heard her sounding adamant about dissolving their marriage. She was set on making it happen, and these six months were only a stumbling block to her. A part of him had hoped that she would be more open to reconsider their relationship. Not for the sake of love or anything so romantic, but because it would be easier on their child. Although his parents hadn't lived to see him today, they had given him a happy, stable family life prior to his leaving for college. He didn't know the type of man he'd be without knowing that kind of love and dedication.

He wanted the same for his son or daughter. And when he pictured that, he couldn't see a life without Zaynab by his side.

Telling her all of this would probably just push her further along the path of divorce. If he wanted this, he'd have to approach the subject carefully, and not right then when she was smiling again and beautifully if not a little sadly.

"I know you might not understand, but it would break her heart to know that we're planning to end things." Zaynab opened the balcony doors and walked out, gripping the iron railing, and heaved a sigh that wasn't entirely despondent. "This place *is* really like a palace. I would be so lucky to call it my home."

"Good, because it is yours."

"What?" Zaynab rounded sharply on him, the pretty view of this affluent neighborhood forgotten. "What do you mean 'it's mine'?"

"The transfer of ownership isn't official until you sign off and have a solicitor notarize it, which I could help you seek out."

She stared at him speechlessly.

Unnerved by her quietness, Ara curled his fingers through his beard. Had he displeased her?

"I can't accept this," she said with a slow shake of her head.

"Why not?"

Her eyes widened, and she looked at him as though he'd asked the obvious. "Because I just can't, Ara. It's too much."

"It's a gift," he intoned.

"It's a *house*. A very big, very expensive house."

He could tell there was more to her reason for not accepting the transfer of ownership than what she was saying, but since he couldn't pry the whole truth out of her, Ara settled on appealing to her senses.

"It's also a part of your mahr." As part of the marriage contract they'd both signed, he and Zaynab had agreed to a contractual dowry that he'd pay if they were to ever divorce. And now that that was looking like more of a reality, Ara had zero intention of depriving her of what he'd promised her. "It's my obligation to you, and the house should satisfy it."

When she still didn't budge, he moved in closer to her—as close as he dared to risk a whiff of her honeyed oud fragrance, then after lowering the hand lazily combing through his beard, he fished the house key from inside of his coat pocket.

The key itself wouldn't be needed to enter the house. Not when he would soon have the home equipped with state-of-the-art biometric locks. But for now the key was symbolic of the house's true owner.

"Take the key, Zaynab." He held it out to her.

"I don't know what to say," she murmured, the indecisiveness still playing out over her beautiful face.

Taking her hand gently, he turned her palm up and settled the key in her grip and closed her fingers around it.

"There's nothing more to say," he told her.

He let her go, not expecting her to raise her other hand and touch his cheek—

Ara jerked back from her.

Zaynab pulled away too. "The scar…"

"What about it?" he heard how gruff he sounded and hated that he'd revealed more emotion in that moment than every other time with her. And considering the way the last time he let his feelings out to play had resulted in her pregnant, Ara rather preferred not being emotional.

"It's healed well, that's all." A beat of silence throbbed between them and then she quietly wondered, "Does it hurt you?"

"No."

"May I?" She lifted her hand again, and damn it, but he couldn't deny her.

He wasn't too bothered by the scar before, but lately, ever since he'd returned from Mauritius and knew that she awaited him in London to start a life with him, Ara had grown obsessed with the physical disfigurement. It represented a time when he'd been at his second most vulnerable, when the explosion that had rocked the hotel he had booked in Mogadishu was bombed randomly. The first time was when his university administrators had pulled him aside and informed him that he had lost his parents.

Growing the beard hadn't been purposeful, but once he looked in the mirror and saw less of the scar, he liked it.

She traced her finger over the old wound gently, following the puckered lighter line from where it started at the top of his cheekbone, right below his eye, and slashing down to just above his lower jawbone. He expected her to stop where his beard concealed that larger, lower portion of the scar, but Zaynab kept moving down, her fingertip softly tickling him and raising goose bumps over his arms.

"You're growing your beard?"

Hearing the question in her voice, he grunted affirmatively, unable to do more than that.

"It looks good," she praised.

She slid her finger up and then cupped his cheek, her thumb smoothing over the scar gently. He closed his eyes and swallowed down the growl rumbling through his chest. God, was she doing this to drive him to madness and beyond? As strong-willed as he could be, it was taking a Herculean effort not to give in to the sheer sinful temptation she posed him right then. But he *couldn't* kiss her. He couldn't lower his head and remind himself of how she tasted. He. Just. Couldn't.

"Ara." She spoke his name on a breathy little whisper before leaning closer.

Gritting his teeth from the sheer force of self-restraint, he had a flash of déjà vu when they were in such a position.

Maybe it was a good thing then that a dog began barking loudly and sharply from one of the nearby terraced houses.

"If you ever need to talk to someone," she said, and drew her hand away and stole the chance of kissing her from him.

Ara tightened his lips but nodded. He probably never would, and yet knowing her offer was available made him hotter for her. That certainly wasn't the way he should feel about the wife that was determined to divorce him.

The wife who was carrying his precious baby.

And the wife who might have almost just kissed him, and whom he certainly would've kissed back.

CHAPTER SIX

A FEW WEEKS ago Ara wouldn't have pictured himself idling in his car in the middle of London while waiting on Zaynab to finish up working and meet him outside.

And yet also a few weeks ago he hadn't thought he'd be a father.

Hadn't ever imagined that he would be excited to meet his son or daughter.

But here he was, looking at his copy of the ultrasound that Zaynab had gifted him and stroking the small pale face in utter awe at the life he'd helped create. A life that would rely on him to protect it.

Ara gritted his teeth as fear prickled his scalp.

Every day brought him boundless joy but also a creeping doubt that he wouldn't be able to keep his family together. And what happened when the doubt eclipsed the happy moments he had thus far shared with Zaynab on this journey of parenthood?

She pushes me out of her and the baby's lives.

Ara tucked the ultrasound back into his wallet, his mind stormier now. A knock on his car window made him realize he had zoned out and missed Zaynab's arrival. Quickly unlocking the car door for her, he braced himself as a rush of wintry air flooded in with her. She dropped back into the passenger seat and heaved a long drawn-out but contented sigh, reaching out and hovering her hands over the car heater.

"That feels so good. It's nearly the end of February and it's still freezing," she groused, shivering and rubbing her hands up and down her arms. "I hope you weren't waiting too long."

He shook his head. "I only just got here." It was a lie; he'd left early to avoid any traffic. He didn't want her waiting in the cold for him, not when he volunteered to give her the rides to and from her workplace.

"And you're still good to go shopping? Because the fridge is dangerously close to empty, and the pantry's getting near there too."

Ara started the engine and pulled out before replying, "Of course, we can't have Button going hungry."

Zaynab snorted. "Forget Button. Mama's hungry," she joked.

"Let's eat dinner first then. The groceries can wait."

Just as he began interpreting the stretch of silence from her to mean she wasn't interested in his offer of dinner, she said, "Are you sure? Because I'd rather not take up more of your time. I feel bad enough when you pick me up. You know I could just take a couple of buses and the tube."

"It's no bother for me to drive you around, and I might as well familiarize myself with the city."

"Okay, but you'll let me know if you ever change your mind."

He wouldn't be doing that ever, and yet seeing that she wanted confirmation for her peace of mind, Ara dipped his chin. "You'll be the first to know if that happens. Now, how about you tell me how your day went."

The remainder of the drive was filled with Zaynab giving him a play-by-play of her eventful day working with her elderly client, Opaline. He listened while she told him about the salacious gossip at the high tea party that she helped host with Opaline for a gaggle of the older woman's friends. She drew rumbling laughter from him a couple of times, and he carried the easygoing mood into a busy East London fast-food eatery.

"We might not find a seat," Zaynab warned, turning to look at him over her shoulder when she was pushed back against him by a couple rowdy teenagers play-fighting in line in front of them.

Settling his hands over her shoulders to steady her against him, Ara made eye contact with the teens and glared menacingly enough for them to straighten up after a quick apology. Satisfied that they wouldn't continue their horseplay, he looked down at where his hands still gripped her. She had her back pressed to his front, the soft dip between her waist and wide hips temptingly within reach, and her body heat seeping through his button-down shirt and awakening his ever-present desire for her.

Being attracted to his wife wasn't a problem, but it would complicate their arrangement. Reminding himself that Zaynab wanted their divorce to still happen was a good way to cool his overheated blood.

Once he was able to do that, taking his hands off her and putting some fraction of space between them was easier.

"Let's go someplace else," she suggested.

He quietly obliged, and they strolled back out onto the high street where they had a wide and varied selection of restaurants and cafés to choose from. Zaynab picked for them again, and he didn't argue.

Unfortunately, this restaurant was just as overpacked as the other one had been.

"We're not having much luck, are we?" she said with a soft groan.

"We don't have to wait to eat. There's always the option of food delivery," he said after seeing the way she rubbed her stomach. He didn't want her going hungry on his watch.

"All right, I guess we can do takeout," Zaynab agreed. "It might be a long while before we're seated."

Ara shadowed her as she turned to leave the restaurant, his hand instinctively settling over the small of her back. She'd already nearly been toppled over by unruly kids in the other restaurant; he didn't want a repeat performance of that as the dinner rush seemed to be striking every eating establishment within walking distance.

Zaynab had almost reached the exit with him by her side when her name being called stopped them both.

A smiling woman in a hot-pink hijab and mustard-yellow blazer and trousers was beelining their way. "Zaynab! It is you!" she exclaimed and threw her arms around her before Ara could react. He would've assessed the woman as a threat if Zaynab hadn't gasped and hugged her back tightly.

"Oh, my goodness, Neelima," Zaynab said, pulling back and grabbing her friend's hands.

"How long has it been? And when did you get back from working in America?"

Grinning, Neelima pulled her left hand out of Zaynab's grasp and flashed it so that the diamond ring was hard to miss.

Zaynab's loud, exalted gasp drew heads their direction.

Squealing together, the two women hugged again.

"We've been married six months now, but my husband's job brought him here about a month ago. We still haven't found a place of our own, so we're living nearby at my parents' place."

Ara gave up following the conversation after that, instead waiting for Zaynab to finish catching up with her friend. He looked around to ensure no other surprises sprang up on them. When he looked at Zaynab, he smiled at seeing her glowing expression of happiness. And he was caught staring at her by both Zaynab and her friend.

"Who's this?" her friend asked, the smile she gave him more restrained and polite.

"My husband, Ara." Zaynab said it so easily it surprised him, especially given their divorce was still very much the elephant in the room with them.

"You're married too!" Neelima clapped her hands happily, and both she and Zaynab giggled together. Then came the shower of questions from her friend. How long had they been married? How did they meet? Was it love at first sight?

Zaynab answered most but that last query. Her friend Neelima didn't notice, her curiosity about his and Zaynab's relationship seemingly sated, but Ara wondered what it meant that Zaynab hadn't responded.

And now that he was thinking about it, had it been love at first glance for him?

Meeting Zaynab wasn't anything he'd planned. Her father orchestrated it, first approaching Ara about a possible marriage match. Of course Sharmarke hadn't disclosed that the match was with his daughter and only child from his first marriage. Not until Zaynab was standing before Ara on their first date aboard his yacht. He'd taken one look at her on his ship's deck, the blue ocean as her backdrop and her pretty face and white abaya awash in the orange glow of sunset, and he'd been as close to smitten as he could be...

He could pretend that he'd been searching for love, but the truth was Ara hadn't cared about any of that. In the beginning his sole motivation in agreeing to a blind date with Zaynab was to lower Sharmarke's guard and get closer to his dark secrets. It had been around that time that Ara had started digging into his father-in-law, and he'd been getting nowhere until Sharmarke started trying to matchmake him.

He still had no clue what her father's motivation had been for playing matchmaker, though if he had to guess Sharmarke had been thinking the same thing and had wanted to spy on him. Not just spy but ensure that he wasn't getting closer to unearthing the truth about his criminal activities. And if that was true, Ara was to blame as he'd provoked her father's suspicion when he had first tried to ask Sharmarke about the heinous crimes he had committed and tried to cover up.

All of it dredged up ugly memories that he had worked to put behind him over the course of the past year. Still, Ara often pondered what Zaynab's life might have been like had he not endeavored to unmask Sharmarke's misdeeds.

We might not have ever met.

And their baby certainly wouldn't exist.

His throat worked around the hard knot that manifested at the awful thought. He swallowed it down when Zaynab's friend walked away and she turned to him with a bright smile.

"Looks like our table might be ready." Zaynab pointed to the host beckoning them to the back of the bistro.

"So, this is where you grew up."

Zaynab masked her smile at Ara's terribly

concealed curiosity. Since he'd discovered this was her old neighborhood, he hadn't stopped looking around with a gleam of intrigue in his eyes. He had barely touched his dinner, his spoon suspended over his red lentil soup, his food taking a back seat to his interest in her.

A familiar skitter of thrill electrified her as his dark eyes bore into her.

Once she would have loved to have this attentive version of him all to herself, and though she appreciated that he was trying now, a part of her remained vigilant and suspicious. It wouldn't be the first time someone in her life had lulled her into believing that they had turned over a new leaf for the better. It had happened with Sharmarke—and it could be happening with Ara right now. Still, even as she considered that possibility, she couldn't help but hope that she was wrong.

That Ara wasn't tricking her like her father had done, and that he actually cared for her more than he was letting on.

Pushing aside her muddled thoughts, she munched on a fermented cauliflower, the comfort from the sour and salty burst of flavor settling her nerves.

And she was glad for it when Ara tipped his head slightly to the side and asked, "Will you tell me about your upbringing?"

Zaynab nodded, wariness creeping over her, the amusement she'd felt earlier at his curiosity now gone.

"What would you like to know?"

"Whatever you're comfortable sharing with me," he said and set down the spoon he had drifting over his still untouched soup.

Surprisingly that calmed her far greater than she would've thought, mostly because one glimpse into those dark pools of his eyes and she knew that he hadn't said it merely as comfort. He was allowing her to take full control of the narrative. Besides her father, she couldn't name another man who was as self-possessed as Ara, and so utterly in charge of not only every aspect of his life but that of the people around him.

After all, he'd talked her into living with him again. But he also hadn't given her a reason to regret that decision so far.

Zaynab smiled at that.

Ara's kissable full lips lifted in response, the corners of his mouth curling up ever so subtly, the warmth of the gesture touching the lightless depths of his eyes. As great as it was to have his attention exclusively to herself, even more than that Zaynab decided she liked his smile.

"Okay," she said slowly, "but, fair warning, I might end up rambling on."

With the way Ara continued to look at her, riveted on her every word, she surmised that he hadn't changed his mind about hearing her tell of her childhood.

She started from the beginning, when she and her mother had first moved from their big, manor-like home in Hargeisa to London, the culture shock alone had almost been too much.

"I hadn't wanted to leave my friends, my home…" *I didn't even want to leave Sharmarke.* Because there had been a time when she'd loved her father so very dearly and couldn't understand how she could live apart from him. "I was ten, so it just felt like my whole world fell apart overnight, and I was powerless to do anything about fixing it."

She paused to savor another pickled vegetable, a carrot this time.

"For the first few months, all I remember was begging my mum to take us home, and when that didn't work, I asked her to send me back alone. Back to Sharmarke because I was sure that he was missing us too. That he was missing me.

"But when those months had passed, and I heard nothing from my father, I started to accept that my mother might have been protecting me from the harsh truth: that Sharmarke wasn't missing us at all, and that he had wanted us out of his life."

She hurtled into the painful memories of her mother scrimping and saving her pay from a number of low-wage jobs to make ends meet, the disrepair of their low-cost housing, and the awkward readjustment to a new life that was especially hard on her when she'd been so young.

"I felt so out of touch with my classmates who were so far ahead in their English studies, and everything around me was so alien," Zaynab recalled.

"Sharmarke sent us money, but it was never enough. Not for the rent, for the groceries, my schoolbooks and supplies and the English tutoring I needed on the side."

Across the table, Ara's brow grooved with deeply disapproving lines, his scowl darkening as her story unfolded. He interlaced his fingers together and, with his elbows on the table, he steepled his hands under his bearded chin. His look urged her to continue.

She didn't think she had it in her, not around the bile curdling in her throat at the mention of how her so-called father had treated her and her mother, but she pushed on.

"The only thing that made it better was our next-door neighbors. My best friend, Salma, her parents and her five siblings."

If it hadn't been for Salma and her family, Zaynab didn't know how her life might have ended up.

"Besides helping us settle in and navigate our new life in the UK, Salma's parents would help my mum translate documents from Somali to English for the immigration offices. They would look after me while my mum would go off to work one of her night shifts, and they'd never treat me any differently than one of their own children. And Salma helped me a lot through school."

She couldn't ever repay them for their kindness to her and her mother. More than that, while Zaynab had lost her father, she had ended up gaining a whole bunch of new family members in Salma's family. She wished that it was completely enough for her; that Sharmarke's abandonment wasn't a sore subject for her, that she felt nothing but indifference.

But she'd never fully understand why her own father hadn't wanted her.

Not that that was Ara's problem. Figuring she'd probably spoiled his mood for dinner, Zaynab looked up and startled at the menacing scowl on his face.

She gulped and stammered, "W-well, I didn't expect for that to get so serious. I'm sorry if I ruined our dinner."

"You have nothing to be sorry for." His fingers flexed and tightened under his chin. "If I possessed the power to punish your father for those specific crimes against you, I would."

And in that moment, in the face of the pure anger storming over his handsome features, Zaynab truly believed he would have. She even suspected that he was playing out exactly how he'd inflict the punishment on Sharmarke. Her stomach turned over and, shaking her head clear of unpleasant images of torture, she smiled weakly.

"As much as I appreciate that offer, I think he's already been punished enough." Multiple life sentences in prison in return for all the damage his political greed caused his victims seemed a fair enough sanction. And she hoped that her father was taking his criminal charges seriously and reflecting on his moral failings.

She bit her lip thoughtfully, not sure if she should ask the question in her head, but then gave in to the drilling need to know. "Was Sharmarke like that with you? I know that he was a friend of your parents."

"No, he never showed that cruel side of himself to us."

The fact that Ara had answered quickly and with no hesitation only proved what she'd always suspected: that her father cared more about her husband than he ever had her. Zaynab knew that Sharmarke was proud of Ara and his many professional achievements. From the moment he'd first mentioned arranging a marriage for her, Sharmarke had spoken highly of Ara.

And though his almost father-like pride for Ara was obvious, so was Sharmarke's fear of him. It became particularly apparent when they had flown to Mogadishu in a hurry when news of Ara's accident there had reached them in Berbera. While she'd been worried that Ara would never recover from his traumatic brain injury or wake from his medically induced coma, Sharmarke had wrung his hands outside Ara's hospital room and had fretted about what secrets Ara had uncovered about him.

"I don't know who got into his ear, but now he believes I'm capable of evil. He wants to ruin me—shame me!" Sharmarke had griped to her, the memory of him pacing back and forth across Ara's private hospital room, sweat glistening on his brown brow and his white teeth bared at the very real threat Ara posed him still very sharp in her mind.

It wasn't the first time she was hearing of Ara spying on him.

"I need to know what he knows, and I need you to tell me," her father had instructed her after pulling her away from some of her

mother's relatives at her and Ara's nikah. Using the pretense of taking special father-daughter photos, he'd found a secluded spot to grasp her shoulders tightly and make the request of her. *No, not a request*, she corrected. He had basically demanded for her to spy on her new husband. *"You're my daughter. My flesh and blood despite what poison your hooyo might have leaked into your ears. I'm the reason you've even married, so you owe me this."*

Zaynab hadn't known what to think, or who to believe was the wrong party—Ara or Sharmarke. She could've asked Ara about it now, but she didn't know what Pandora's box that line of questioning would open, especially when they'd been doing so well living together.

She wouldn't allow Sharmarke to wreck that for her. He'd caused her enough emotional harm to last her a lifetime and more.

Sadness clanged in her at that truth, and on impulse, she reached for her plate of pickled vegetables to soothe the ache in her soul, at least until her fingers scraped over the empty plate.

Before she could sulk too much, Ara placed his side of pickled vegetables by her.

"I'll likely not touch them," he said when she tried refusing.

"Oh, okay. Thanks." Popping fermented

cabbage into her mouth, Zaynab squeezed her eyes shut and moaned in sheer culinary delight. When her eyes landed back on Ara, she blushed, realizing she'd allowed her pleasure to run away with her. "Sorry, I've been craving pickles more than usual. I think it's the pregnancy cravings because I could probably just eat heaps of the fermented vegetables alone and call it a night."

After that, their dinner resumed more quietly but peacefully. Other than a few comments about their delicious Middle Eastern dishes, Zaynab didn't mind that Ara was mostly silent.

In fact the next time he spoke was when their bill was delivered and Ara refused for her to pay.

"I ate way more than you did," she argued.

"And that's because you're carrying my baby," he said.

He made a good point, but she still conceded with a little huff.

Adding an extremely generous tip, and with a half-crooked smirk smacking of his victory, Ara stood and walked away to deliver their fully paid bill in person.

Unable to help herself, Zaynab followed him with her eyes. The tailored cut of his blazer molded to those broad shoulders of his, and his trousers hugged his backside perfectly and had her grateful that she was seated when her legs weakened on her.

Needing a distraction before she melted into a goopy puddle, she whipped out her phone and scrolled her apps aimlessly until a text from Salma popped up.

"Ready to leave?"

At the sound of his voice, Zaynab snapped her head up to Ara and then fixed her sights on the large jar of pickled vegetables in his hands. Not giving her a chance to ask, he explained, "I figured it would save some time rather than calling in and ordering when you had a craving."

She couldn't deny that the sight of the jar already had her drooling.

Ara then looked pointedly at her phone. "Did you want to finish writing your message?"

"Yes, if you don't mind. Salma just texted to ask if I'd still want to have our first iftar together. It's sort of a tradition for us." It started after she and Salma both moved together to enroll at the University of Edinburgh. Between Salma's nursing courses and her work placements in the Health in Social Science program, going home for all of Ramadan hadn't been a viable option for either of them. Like her, Zaynab knew that Salma looked forward to iftar together every year.

But she was stuck on a response. With Ramadan less than a week away, and Ara being with her this year, it naturally made sense for her to spend that time with him.

He seemed to understand her dilemma. "Why not invite her over?" he proposed.

Concealing her surprise, Zaynab hedged, "You wouldn't mind?"

Ara frowned down at her, looking adorably baffled. "Why would I mind? She's a close friend of yours, and it's Ramadan. Spending quality time with family, friends and community is a hallmark of the holiday."

Huh. She didn't take him for someone who really cared. When she'd first lived with him, she hadn't met any of Ara's friends. As for his family, though Sharmarke had already told her of the sad fate of Ara's parents, Zaynab had heard he had a sister and expected to meet her. But at their nikah, he had informed her his little sister, Anisa, lived abroad in Canada and was too indisposed to attend their nuptials.

"And anyway, your friend will be around our baby. I should meet her."

Zaynab grinned. *That* was more like the excessively cautious man she married.

Now she just had to wonder whether Ara would carry that suspicion with him when Salma came over for dinner, and if he even understood what he'd gotten himself into by giving Zaynab permission to officially introduce him to her outspoken best friend.

CHAPTER SEVEN

WHEN ARA AGREED to meeting Zaynab's friend Salma, he had seen the opportunity for what it was: a chance to get to know his wife and the mother of his child better. Living with Zaynab this past month had been enlightening, but that short time couldn't give him the same insight that her best friend of over twenty years could, and so he was looking forward to their iftar meal with Salma tonight.

And this was despite Zaynab teasing, "Are you sure you're ready for this?"

"Only if you are," he said with confidence. How hard could sitting through a few questions from her friend be?

"Famous last words," she whispered, snickering. Her snicker cut short when he came up behind her while she set up their tableware for the evening. With his chest nearly touching her back, he held out the soup spoons she'd forgotten, and watched her transform into the portrait of shyness as she accepted the spoons from him and avoided his eyes.

Amused by this swift change in her, Ara cleared his throat and once she braved looking at him, he said, "We're going to have a good dinner."

"I'm sure you'll win her over with your food. I still can't believe you didn't tell me you could cook."

His chuckle only gained him a swat on the arm from her.

"Seriously, where did you learn how to make all this?" Zaynab swept her hand toward the kitchen where varied dishes rested on plate warmers for their first iftar meal.

It wasn't that Ara kept that part of him secret, but before this night there was little time in his scheduling to cook as much as he'd like. Since moving in with Zaynab, he'd adopted more of a work-life balance, and that freed him up to not only spend time with her, but to help prepare dinner for her good friend.

And he should thank her. He'd forgotten how rewarding it could be to cook for someone else and watch as they delighted in his culinary talents. There weren't a lot of people in his life now that cared about that part of him. His parents certainly hadn't, not when he'd told them that he was considering taking a year off from his business program to apprentice with a well-renowned Somali chef who he'd admired. They'd nurtured his abilities in the kitchen up until that point. Then suddenly, almost overnight, his mother and father threatened to retract their financial support.

"Someone has to run our business someday," his mother had urged.

"You're our son. Naturally, it has to be you," insisted his father.

Ara stiffened his limbs as their voices echoed down the chambers of his long memory. He didn't like to think of them in that light. Didn't like the way that version of his parents made him forget how much he missed them.

Unlike his mother and father, Zaynab clearly was interested, given the way she'd happily volunteered to taste test all of his dishes. Now she was looking at him and waiting patiently for his explanation.

Just as he opened his mouth to answer her, the doorbell rang.

"Well, that's her," Zaynab announced with a sigh and a smile. "Too late to back out now."

He had the sense that she wasn't just taunting him anymore. This dinner had to be far more important than she'd let on.

Ara didn't have any friends that were close enough for their opinions to matter to him, at least he didn't any longer. He sympathized with her because he imagined it was how he'd feel with Anisa and Zaynab meeting—an event that had yet to happen. And when that happened, he knew he'd be sweating bullets worrying about whether his sister and wife would get along. Put like that then, it was fair that Zaynab was anxious about him meeting her friend.

Ignoring the doorbell chiming a second time, Ara reached for her arm and stopped Zaynab on her way to the door.

"Everything will be all right." He moved from gripping her arm to taking her hand and giving her a squeeze he hoped communicated comfort.

Smiling and appearing more relaxed, she squeezed his hand back.

Then she slipped free of him and went to answer the door at the chirp of the third and final doorbell.

"About time, babes," he heard Salma drawl before she stepped in and pulled Zaynab down to hug her. He couldn't get much of an impression of her until Zaynab ushered Salma in from the cold and closed the front door.

Side by side, the two women couldn't be more different.

Though Zaynab had been in the kitchen with him for a long while now, she had just pulled off her apron and set it aside. Now he could fully appreciate her lush curves in a café au lait–colored tunic and trouser set, her feet shod in fuzzy black slippers, her hair free of her hijab and drawn up into a high sleek ponytail, and her makeup enhancing the naturally alluring glow of her rich brown skin. Salma was shorter by half a foot, though she wore knee-high boots with the tallest heels he'd ever seen. She was also slender and her big dark curly hair puffed around a small heart-shaped face. Shrugging out of her coat and letting Zaynab take it and walk away to hang it up, her friend stood in a long sweater dress and a fuzzy faux fur vest, looking approachable enough outwardly until she turned up her nose and pinned him with a frosty look.

Waiting in awkward silence for Zaynab to return, Ara witnessed Salma blink and resume a neutral expression. As though she hadn't just been glaring daggers at him.

"Have you two met yet?" Zaynab asked sweetly and looked between them.

Ara reminded himself that this meant a lot to her, and that it didn't matter how many dark looks Salma slung his way, they were both there because they cared for Zaynab. If he had to be the bigger person, then he would take that high road proudly and quietly.

* * *

It wasn't that Zaynab had believed dinner with Salma would be quiet, uneventful—peaceful even. She'd just *prayed* that it would be. But from the minute her friend walked in and met Ara, any semblance of hope escaped Zaynab.

Salma had sharpened her long nail extensions to do battle and defend her, whether Zaynab wanted it or not. And her choice of weapon? Silent treatment. She ignored Ara, first giving him the cold shoulder while he and Zaynab gave her a tour of their home and then again when they were seated in the living room to wait out the final few minutes until their first day of fasting ended. Not knowing if Ara had sensed Salma's passive-aggressive attitude toward him, and whether that was why he deferred to her to do the talking, Zaynab sat between them and carried the conversation as cheerfully as she could given their awkward situation.

She was glad then when the call to Maghreb prayer sounded from her phone. She had set the reminder so that they wouldn't miss breaking their fast, but first she passed dates around for them to eat and poured them glasses of water.

After Ara led her and Salma in prayer, they gathered for iftar in the dining room.

Although Zaynab was famished, with the stifling atmosphere hanging over them, she found it difficult to enjoy the delicious dinner that Ara had worked hard to make them.

Salma continued to ignore him for the most part, except when she was forced to interact with him. Once because he was closest to the small bowl of basbaas, a green hot sauce, a staple in Somali cuisine, and another time when she complimented Zaynab on the shami kebab after doling out seconds onto her dinner plate.

"I would love to take the praise, but I'm not the chef," Zaynab said to her with a smile and nod at Ara.

"I see," was all she said to that, her lips thinned in displeasure for a long time after. Zaynab even noticed Salma didn't go back for thirds either.

Once they were finished with their dinner, and looking far more exhausted than he should have, Ara offered to clear the table and fetch their dessert. That left Zaynab to usher Salma back toward the sitting room. Once she was certain that Ara couldn't hear them, she rounded on her friend with a glare.

"You promised you'd be nice," she reminded her. Worried that Salma might act like this, Zaynab had called and warned her earlier to bring an open mind with her to their intimate dinner party.

Salma huffed, "But I *am* being nice…"

Not believing that for a second, Zaynab arched a brow, and Salma groaned and flopped back onto the sofa cushions, arms crossed in petulant rebellion.

"Okay! Fine, I'm not being nice at all." Salma scowled. "Why should I be though? He's the reason I didn't even get to take time off work and celebrate your nikah in Berbera."

Zaynab smiled as Salma pouted childishly. "You know that I agreed to the fast deadline for our marriage." When Ara had proposed, she hadn't seen a reason for them to be engaged for long. She was so sure she loved him—so very certain in her choice to be his bride that she hadn't ever thought their marriage would be at risk of falling apart...

And it was hard not to be reminded of it when Salma argued, "All right, but when you first came back a year ago, you were so unhappy. I hated that he made you sad. Give me one good reason why I should play nice after that."

"Because Ara spent all day slaving away in the kitchen, making our dinner. I told him about our iftar tradition, and I think he wanted to make this first day memorable for us both. Also, he's been looking forward to meeting you." Zaynab rattled off the long list of good deeds, surprised at how quickly heated she'd become on Ara's behalf.

She told herself that it was because he didn't deserve Salma's poor treatment when he'd been nothing but polite in return.

And maybe I want Salma to see this version of him that I'm seeing... This sweet, thoughtful, and highly attentive version of Ara who Zaynab could see herself living with, not just for the remaining five months of their six-month agreement, but maybe, *possibly* maybe forever.

She startled at that thought.

Was that what she wanted now instead of the divorce? To live with Ara permanently, raise their baby in this home they were building together, and even try at saving their marriage?

Zaynab shook her head, bewildered at where her thinking had gone.

And she wasn't alone in the confusion.

Eyes as wide as saucers, Salma unfolded her arms and sat up ramrod straight.

"Zaynab, you... You really sound like you care about him."

It was Zaynab's turn to frown. Still confused, she shrugged her shoulders and pressed both her hands over the fluttering in her lower belly. "Well, I have to, don't I? He's the father of my child."

"No, not like that," Salma interjected, leaning in and studying her with narrowed eyes. "I mean, you *care* for him."

"I said I did."

"You like him!" goaded Salma.

Blushing to the tips of her ears, Zaynab snapped her head to the entrance of the sitting room in case Salma's voice had carried.

"Yes, I like him, but not in the way you're thinking. Now, hush, I hear him coming back."

But not letting it go completely, Salma winked at her, mimed zipping her lips and grinned impishly. "Uh-huh. Okay. Whatever you say. My lips are sealed."

"Oh, just be nice, all right?" Salma could wind her up all she wanted, but Zaynab was drawing the line with her attitude when it came to Ara.

And Salma seemed to take her warning to heart. Seemingly oblivious to being the subject of their conversation, Ara carried in a tray of frozen chocolate dessert he'd baked himself and cups of tea, and Salma accepted her slice of cake and tea from him with a smile and a friendly enough "Ta!"

He looked visibly taken aback for a moment before his usual brooding mask fell into place.

Zaynab ducked her head to hide her smile, relieved when the conversation flowed more naturally after that. It wasn't perfect by any standard, but at least Salma was attempting to be polite this time. She asked Ara about his business and culinary skills and how he liked his stay in London, and though her questions and his answers weren't indicative of them ever becoming friends, the evening ended on a far more hopeful note than it had begun.

All except for a small speed bump that happened when Salma was heading out.

Zaynab walked her to the front door, with Ara trailing behind them closely.

Salma confirmed her rideshare was there and, insisting that they didn't walk her outside, she crushed Zaynab in a hug. When she let her go, Salma narrowed her eyes sharply and suddenly to where Ara stood and pointed a finger at him.

"You make sure you don't do anything to hurt her or the baby, otherwise you'll have me to answer to, mister."

"I would hurt myself first rather than hurt her."

Zaynab's heart thudded at the darkly stern conviction in his words.

Apparently having seen something in his expression that made her believe his words, Salma bobbed her head firmly and then, blowing an air kiss at Zaynab, she opened the door and left.

Zaynab stood frozen in shock, surprised at what had transpired around her, and she didn't move until Ara passed her to lock the front door and secure the house alarm.

"Why do I get the sense you two are conspiring against me?"

He smiled. "I don't think *conspiring* is the right word. We both merely share a vested interest in your and Button's safety."

She followed him to the kitchen and jumped in when he started loading the dishwasher. After they'd done that, he turned to wash the remaining overflow of dishes in the double sink.

"I'm sorry if Salma came off as, well, *forceful*." Zaynab peeked over at him but found his facial expression offered her no hint of what he was thinking. "Dinner wasn't so bad though... Right?"

"No, it wasn't awful," he said with a shrug.

"Wait. What was that?"

Ara flicked her a quick glance. "What was what?"

"That little shrug." She mimicked it for him, her heart thumping as she wondered, "Did you not like Salma?"

He set down the sudsy plate he'd been cleaning, washed his hands and twisted the tap closed before he looked at her.

"I know why it matters to you that I like her, but at the end of the day she's your friend. My liking her or not shouldn't change your opinion of her."

"That doesn't answer my question."

Sighing, Ara rubbed a hand over his beard.

"It's okay. I won't get upset, promise. I just want to know what you think of her."

"Very well. She's rude," he said, surprising her with his abruptness.

Even though that was a fair summarization of how Salma acted, Zaynab opened her mouth, ready to defend her friend.

But Ara continued, "I also now know that she cares deeply for your well-being, and it eases my mind to know that you have her by your side. Between Salma and your mother, you'll have plenty of support for when the baby comes. At least after you tell your mother of the pregnancy. You might not even need me…"

He said the last part quietly, almost resignedly, before he lowered his hand from combing through his beard and turned back to wash the dishes.

Zaynab clamped her lips together, not knowing what to say after his statement.

All she knew was that the need to embrace Ara was so overwhelming, she wrapped her arms around her middle to avoid the instinct to hug and pour comfort into him.

Why would he think that she wouldn't need him?

She remained puzzled as to where he'd gotten

that idea until she wiped the last of the dishes he'd finished washing, then it struck her swiftly.

It's my fault!

When she looked at it from his perspective, it was easy to understand where his sudden irrelevancy sprang from. First, she had initiated their talk of divorce. Though she didn't regret asking to end their marriage, knowing that she needed a clean break at the time, Zaynab had never considered how Ara might have felt and always just assumed he couldn't have cared if she left him because he hadn't seemed to care when they were married.

And more recently she'd requested that her pregnancy and their moving in together be kept a secret from her mother.

If he had done that to her, she would've felt pretty irrelevant too.

She couldn't do anything about the divorce, at least not when she wasn't sure how she felt about their marriage anymore.

But her mother not knowing? That was something she could remedy right then.

They had no sooner finished cleaning up from their dinner when Zaynab picked up her phone.

Ara had no clue what she was up to until she pressed her mobile to her ear, smiled cheerfully and said, "Salaams, Mum!"

She had rung her mother. He was gleaning an idea of where she was going with this, but he didn't expect her to turn on her phone's speaker and set it down on the kitchen peninsula between them.

Her mother jumped into immediately wondering why Zaynab had called so late, the anxiety plain in her voice when she asked in Somali, "Are you okay?"

"Yes, Mum, I'm all right. I've only rung to tell you something," she answered, flashing him a quick smile that just as rapidly flipped over into a frown when he reached over and pressed the mute button on the call.

"You don't have to do this," he said firmly.

"Did you just mute me?" She waved him away and glared when he pulled the phone back as she reached out to unmute the call.

"Hello?" her mother called. "Zaynab, hooyo macaan, are you there?"

"Listen, if you're doing this because you feel pressured to make this announcement, don't."

He didn't want her making a hasty decision to fulfill some obligation to him. *It's my fault though.* If Zaynab felt guilty, it was because he'd gone and opened his mouth and let slip a fear that he'd only begun feeling as of late. A fear that he wasn't needed by her, and not certainly when she was surrounded by the love and support of her mother and friends who were like family to her.

But that was his problem, *his* concern, and Ara hadn't wanted any of it touching Zaynab and their baby.

Of course he'd ended up slipping up and now she possibly felt responsible for his fears and doubts.

Zaynab appeared to understand what he was thinking though.

She wasn't glaring at him anymore, her eyes far softer on him now. "As sweet as that is, I've already made up my mind. Now, my mobile, if you please."

And before her mother hung up, Ara sighed, unmuted the call and handed Zaynab her phone.

"Still here, Mum," she reassured her worried mother. "Like I said, I have something to tell you. Well, *we* have something to tell you. Ara is here with me."

That was his cue to lean in and greet his mother-in-law. She sounded elated, her worry melting into loud, overenthusiastic effusions of maternal care. Ara blushed at all the lavish praise she showered on him.

"Mum, you're giving Ara way more attention than you normally do me. Should I be jealous?" Zaynab teased.

"Why didn't you tell me he was there with

you?" her mother lightly scolded her. "I know you missed him, but I hope you didn't ask him to come over just because of that. That poor boy, I can only imagine the amount of work his business requires of him—"

Visibly flustered, Zaynab groaned, "Mum, stop!" She avoided his eyes and switched her mother off speaker and pressed the phone back to her ear.

Ara stared at her in surprise. Zaynab had… She'd missed him. Why hadn't she ever told him?

Because I never gave her the impression that I cared, and never gave her the attention she deserved.

He had trouble swallowing that truth down as he listened to Zaynab begging her mother to stop embarrassing her. Eventually she turned back to him and, still looking shyly at him, placed the phone down, the speaker back on.

"Okay, Mum, let's try this again," Zaynab said calmly. "The reason Ara is here and the reason we're calling now is because we were waiting to tell you that… That I'm pregnant."

He was wrong if he'd thought her mother had been gushingly loud earlier at discovering that he was with her daughter. The moment she'd learned she was a grandmother-to-be, Zaynab's mother screeched her happiness and threatened to rupture their eardrums in the process. When her mother began ululating like she would at a wedding, Zaynab laughed out loud and wiped tears from the corners of her sparkling eyes, her radiant smile pulling at something deep in him when she looked at him like no one and nothing else existed outside of that special moment. Not the ecstatic shouts of her mother congratulating them, not the memory of Salma warning him before she left and not even the worry that he could cause Zaynab to hurt again.

CHAPTER EIGHT

THOUGH A FULLY grown woman, Zaynab still loved waking up on Eid morning.

When she'd been young, it was the promise of getting money and gifts from the grown-ups in her life, but now, it was the nostalgia she lived for. Well, that and the promise of tearing into a fluffy yellow cambaabur. Served during Eid, the traditional Somali crepe-like pancake was the first thing Zaynab looked forward to on that special day. Her mother made the best cambaabur, though sadly she wouldn't get to glut herself on any this Eid.

Since clearing out their old home in the city seven months ago and moving to her cute little seaside town, Zaynab's mother hadn't returned to London for a visit.

She would have asked for her to come over, but she knew the nearly five-hour journey for her mother would be too exhausting. Despite conquering several rounds of chemo, and enduring plenty of hospital stays, her mother happily being on remission from cancer didn't completely scrub Zaynab's concern for her. So it was out of the question to put her through the kind of travel that might wear her down and undo all her mother's healing progress.

But when Zaynab had hoped to visit her with Ara instead, her mother had insisted over the phone that they not worry themselves with the journey. She cited Zaynab's pregnancy and chided her on traveling when she was in such a delicate state. Arguing with her hadn't worked, mostly because her mother had talked Ara into her line of thinking.

"I know you want to see her, but she could be right. A lengthy car ride won't be comfortable for you, or for Button," he'd said to her after they had gotten off the phone with her mother.

Petty of her, but Zaynab paused brushing her teeth and frowned at her reflection in the bathroom mirror, annoyed still that he hadn't taken her side on the matter. Wasn't he *her* husband? Sure, they might be headed for divorce, but shouldn't their bond count for a little more support?

She knew she was being silly, and that they both only wanted what was best for her and the baby, but it didn't stop her from grumbling about it while getting ready for the Eid activities in store for her and Ara that day.

It wasn't until she was fully dressed and opened her bedroom door that her irritation came to an abrupt halt.

Zaynab sniffed the air and closed her eyes, immediately placing the familiar scent. It was cambaabur, and its freshly baked aroma wafted through the halls and permeated the whole house as she climbed down the floating stairs to the ground floor. It had to be Ara. Since discovering he could seriously cook up a storm, he'd been treating her to scrumptious meals, day and night. Ramadan had always been special to her, but it was made only more so when she was rewarded after a long day of fasting with one of his culinary masterpieces.

And she really shouldn't have expected Eid to bring an end to him delighting her with his food.

Her mouth watering, she followed the divine smells to the kitchen and beamed when she saw Ara's back to her as he stood over the stovetop. Sleeves rolled up and an apron tied around him, he was moving steadily, pouring the yellow batter and working between two frying pans. And judging by the plate of towering, steaming fresh cambaabur behind him on the shiny marble countertop of the kitchen peninsula, he'd been cooking for a while. She would even guess that he'd gotten up at sunrise since it was only a little after seven in the morning.

Ara was so busy toiling at the stove, he hadn't yet noticed her presence.

Zaynab didn't rush to inform him. Seizing the moment to watch him instead, she leaned against the side of the arched entranceway to the kitchen and pressed a hand to her chest, her heart so full knowing that he was working hard to make this Eid meaningful for them.

If she thought about it, it already was pretty momentous. *Because it's our first Eid together.* And not just the two of them, but their baby was technically there too. Zaynab raised her free arm and wrapped it around her stomach, the smile splitting over her face lighting up her insides. She didn't think anything else could make her happier right then. Except she didn't count on Ara glancing over his shoulder at her as he finally realized she was there.

"Good morning," she said with a shy little wave and walked into the kitchen. After pulling out a stool at the peninsula, she sat facing him and tracked his movements as he lowered the dials on the stove and, covering both frying pans with lids, he turned to her.

"Good morning," he rumbled back, his smooth, deep voice rousing a thrilling little shiver from her. He then nudged his chin at the cambaabur and said, "Go ahead and eat without me. I'll join in once I finish up the rest of the batter. Can I get you anything to drink? Tea or yogurt?"

"Yogurt," she said quickly. "Definitely yogurt." She wrinkled her nose at the suggestion of pairing cambaabur with tea.

Like he had the Eid pancakes, Ara whipped up the yogurt drink for her, even stirring in the sugar before he passed the mug over.

"So good," she moaned at her first bite, her eyes nearly rolling back in pleasure. "It even tastes like my mum's."

"That's because it is your mum's."

Zaynab's eyes bulged at his comment, but when she went to open her mouth, the small bite of cambaabur jammed in her throat. She jerked forward and coughed violently and thumped her chest.

Ara was by her side in the blink of an eye, pushing away her cup and plate and patting her back. Together, their efforts dislodged the food and got her breathing easier.

One last thump of her chest and she croaked, "W-what did you just say?"

The smoke detector pealed before he could answer.

Calmly walking over to a security panel, just

one of many scattered throughout the house, Ara pressed in an alphanumeric code, aligned his thumb to a biometric reader and finally silenced the fire alarm.

He then pulled the frying pans off the stove and, prying the lids off, fanned at the thick acrid smoke pluming out at him.

Zaynab was focused on him, and even rose up from her seat to lend a hand, when a new voice floated into the kitchen.

"Have the cambaabur burned?"

"Mum?" Forgetting to help Ara, Zaynab popped out of her stool and onto her feet and stared at her mother like she was seeing a ghost. As shocked as she was to see her, she rushed over and embraced her mother tightly. It was only once the welcoming scent of her mother's favorite bakhoor perfume filled her nose that she didn't think she could ever let go. "Mum, what are you doing here?" she said, still clutching her.

If her mother hadn't peeled her back by the shoulders and kissed her cheeks, Zaynab would have continued clinging to her.

"What do you mean? To celebrate Eid with my beautiful daughter and her handsome husband, of course."

Zaynab stifled her exasperated groan. "Okay, but *how* are you here?" Not that she didn't love the idea. No, she was fighting back happy tears.

Her mother gave her a secretive smile and then tipped her head over Zaynab's shoulder. At Ara.

Understanding slowly, Zaynab turned to him. "You did this?"

"Ara called me a few nights ago, after we had spoken and decided for you to both stay in the city. He told me how much it would mean to you to have me over for Eid."

"Well, he's right," Zaynab agreed, sniffling again and then flicking her watering eyes up to the ceiling with a laugh. "But I don't understand. How did you get here so fast?"

Her mother's eyes twinkled. "I flew on a private plane. A very big, very beautiful plane that my son-in-law sent to me."

"Is this true?" Zaynab spun around to Ara.

He nodded. "It seemed the safest and fastest method."

And now because of him she had her mother with her, and right on time to celebrate Eid.

"I love that you're here, Mum. I've missed seeing your face, and talking over video calls doesn't count."

This time her mother engulfed her in a hug, pulling Zaynab down to her height and rocking her from side to side.

Drawing back, her mother cupped Zaynab's cheeks and smiled, her own eyes glistening with unshed tears. "I missed you too. Now let's stop crying. It's Eid, and we all should be happy."

"But these are happy tears!" Zaynab laughed again and, pulling back from her mother, fanned at her face to stave off the waterworks. When she was positive her makeup wasn't running, she waved for her mother to sit and eat with her. And when her mother asked for some tea with her cambaabur, Zaynab used the excuse of popping on a kettle to sidle up to the stove beside Ara and whisper, "Why didn't you tell me?"

"Your mother made me promise to keep it a secret. In her defense, she wanted to surprise you."

She didn't know which filled her with joy more: that he was defending her mother's reasoning, or that he'd helped orchestrate bringing her mother to her so that they could celebrate Eid together. Never would she have ever imagined that Ara would have done something so sweet for her. At least, she wouldn't have thought him capable of it a couple months ago. But since they'd moved in together again, Zaynab recognized that he was making more room in his overflowing schedule for her. Beyond feeling less and less invisible to him every day, she also no longer felt like a task he could cross off his to-do list, and more like a partner in this marriage that once seemed so utterly doomed to her.

It's everything I wanted from the start.

Everything that was now making her question her previous, possibly hasty impression of him and their unhappy past attempt at living together.

Ara had been keeping a tally of things in his life that had changed since Zaynab reentered his world.

Right off the bat, there was a lot more laughter. Especially now that she was growing comfortable around him. And she'd have to be comfortable to be laughing at him in the background after some older aunties had stopped him outside the masjid following Eid prayer and practically tossed their daughters in front of him.

Extracting himself from them, Ara hurried over to where she stood, a hand clapped to her mouth but her eyes shining their mirth at his expense.

"You could have lent a hand," he grumbled at her, fighting his own smile when she guffawed at him.

"And shatter the hope of those poor aunties? I think not. Besides, I can't imagine you didn't soak up that attention. Come on, admit that you—"

Zaynab gasped as he snaked an arm around her shoulders and pulled in close to her. Ara hadn't meant to cut her off midsentence. It was simply that he'd noticed the aunties had been hovering in the wings, watching his interaction with Zaynab carefully and he hadn't wanted to give them any more hope.

Because even if he and Zaynab divorced, he'd already decided that marriage with anyone else wasn't for him.

From his peripheral vision he could see the brood of aunties collectively sigh in disappointment before scattering through the courtyard—he only presumed in search of eligible bachelors.

Following them with his eyes until he was certain the coast was clear, Ara looked down at Zaynab, the apology ready on his tongue evaporating.

Gawking up at him, her head slightly tipped back, eyes wide and frozen on his face, and her soft-looking painted mouth rounded in astonishment, she had a hand to his chest and the other clutched at the simple gold necklace that echoed the gold threads in her lustrous pink dirac. He didn't normally care for the traditional Somali garb, but on Zaynab, Ara seemed to have unearthed a newfound appreciation.

Even though the dress hung over her loosely

and she wore a blazer that covered most of her top half, the white belt cinched above her swelling belly had taunted him with the hint of womanly curves he knew she possessed. Curves that were now pressing into him and unlocking the desire he kept sealed away for both of their sakes. But wanting Zaynab? That was always simmering below the surface. And with each day that passed together, the temptation of giving in to his lustful urges grew more appealing.

No. I can't do that to her, at least not again.

She'd come to him for a divorce, and what had he done? Seduced her into bed and impregnated her.

Ara ground his teeth at the memory of his barbarism. Though he'd been intensely attracted to her from the very first moment they had met, he had done well to keep it under lock and key for a reason. He was damaged. His confidence broken ever since he'd lost his parents, and his trust was only further abused when Zaynab's father had then gone on to betray him with his crimes. Ara had married her to protect her from the threats her father's criminality might pose her.

So when that threat was locked up with Sharmarke, he'd hoped that he could repair what he might have broken with Zaynab.

But then she'd asked for a divorce, and though

it destroyed that hope he had for their marriage, Ara knew that he'd be doing right by her if he gave her the clean break from him that she clearly yearned for.

It should have been a lesson to him this time around, and a reminder that they were only living together once more for their baby.

That's all that matters now. This baby, and the family the two of us will build around him or her.

But even as he thought this, he didn't make a move to drop his arm off her shoulders or pull away. Instead, he raked his eyes over her, taking in the swell of her breasts as her chest rose and fell rapidly under his stare, then over to where her henna-painted fingers curled into the front gold embroidery of his black thobe.

She appeared as entranced by him as he was spellbound by her.

And despite being in the center of the overly populated sahn outside the masjid, when she sucked in her bottom lip, he was transported back to several months ago, in that hotel room of hers in Berbera. A kiss was what had undone him then—and it was looking like a kiss would be doing it again.

Eyes glued to her mouth, he lowered his head, his heart sounding loudly in his ears and filtering out the Eid merriment filling the masjid's large central courtyard.

A little closer...

An inch or two more.

He could feel her sweet breath puff over his sparking lips, and then—

"Zaynab? Ara?"

Her mother calling out to them jolted him back from her and, simultaneously, saved plenty of unsuspecting witnesses from being scandalized.

Ara dropped his arm off Zaynab and she stepped away, shyly bowing her head and keeping him from seeing her expression.

Zaynab nudged him then. "Come on. I don't want to miss the Eid festival."

As she dragged him along to the festival, her hand on his long, loose sleeve, Ara caught the amused grin stretching his cheeks up.

Zaynab saw it too as she smirked back at him and hauled him along with the Eid crowd spilling out from the masjid and onto the city streets.

Across from the masjid was a park, and though Ara hadn't paid it any mind when they'd arrived at the masjid for Eid prayer, he could now see that the expansive area of greenery hosted an abundance of tents and stalls, and a large central stage for the festival's musical entertainment.

"Hurry!" Zaynab urged, pulling him with her to the heart of the party. "I don't want us missing out on all the fun."

CHAPTER NINE

As THEY SQUEEZED their way through the crowded thoroughfare between stalls and tents, Ara calculated that there must have been hundreds if not thousands of people there. Normally he would've regarded that many people in one area as a viable hazard, and then he'd be expending all his energy on how to minimize said hazard, missing what was in front of him. But right then security risk assessment couldn't be further from his mind.

They took pictures together and then joined the dancing near the stage where a live band played catchy, chart-topping tunes for the crowds. When they'd started slowing down around noon, Zaynab lured him toward a food truck parked nearby, and they hauled fizzy drinks, cheesy chips and gravy and doner kebab to the first empty picnic table they spotted beneath a cluster of early blooming cherry blossoms.

"Having fun?" she asked him, her grin ever present.

He chuckled. "Fun isn't the word I'd use, but it's close." Exhilarating would be more like it. His humor slipped as he recalled when the last Eid he'd celebrated with his parents was, over sixteen years ago. Had he known that his parents would die a couple months later and that would be the final time he'd get to celebrate with them, he wouldn't have dared act the way he had to them.

Banishing the rest of where that memory would take him, Ara blinked free of the past and stared into the unease on Zaynab's pretty face.

"Ara? What's wrong?"

She lowered her fork and swiped her mouth with a napkin, and he hated that she was now frowning because of him.

He could lie to her. Pretend like he wasn't reminded of what he'd lost. But while sitting with her and partaking in the Eid festivities, one look at her knitted brows and the concern shining out of her eyes and he knew that he'd be telling her the truth.

"I was just thinking of my parents and the last Eid we spent together, that's all."

Her hand settled over his atop the picnic table,

communicating quiet sympathy. "Do you mind if I ask about them?"

Ara hesitated, but then he shook his head, realizing that he wasn't as pained by the thought now that she proposed it.

"What were they like?"

Of all the questions, that one was the easiest for him to answer. Smiling, he said, "Thoughtful, generous, nurturing—though we didn't see eye to eye all the time, I counted myself lucky to have them as my parents."

"They started your family's shipping business, right?"

He nodded. "From the ground up. They'd often tell me and Anisa that it was the second most precious thing in their lives, with us being their first." He hung his head, smile vanishing as he swallowed thickly. This was the part he hated talking about, and though he'd never have considered saying anything, delving into the past had loosened his stiff tongue. "They'd always planned for me to take over once I came of age and they'd trained me on everything."

"Why not Anisa?" Zaynab asked the question he'd often wondered himself.

"She's nine years younger, and since I was the oldest and their only son, I became the natural choice of heir for them." And Ara hadn't minded at first, but then that was before he'd gone to board at his university and before he had started discovering his independence and his own dreams.

"You didn't want that," she said, intuiting his mind.

Astonished, Ara recovered and bobbed his head solemnly. "One night, I'd gone to a new restaurant with some friends. The chef and owner was an older local man who had spent many years traveling the globe, and all in the pursuit of his culinary calling. The food he made for us that night," he groaned softly at the memory, licking his lips.

Zaynab laughed. "So, that's who I have to thank for all the good food you've been making me."

"I'd say he was more the spark. After that night, and that experience, I started practicing in the kitchen on my own. My parents were proud especially. They'd often get me to cook when they had company over for dinner. At least they *were* proud until I announced that I wanted to take a year's break from my business program. Then, almost overnight, they retracted their support."

Zaynab squeezed his hand. "I'm sorry that happened to you."

There was more he could have said, but Ara left it at, "Even though I couldn't see it fully

then, I now understand where they were coming from. They were just worried about what
would happen to their business legacy.

"And after they died, it seemed the natural
course for me to take up their mantle." More
than that it had felt imperative to him. Like if
he worked hard on the company's behalf, toiled
in enough sweat and sacrificed enough of his
personal life, that he'd make amends to them.

That they'd forgive him wherever they were.

That I'd be able to forgive myself...

"The first Eid without them, I tried for
Anisa's sake to be cheery and normal."

"But you couldn't," Zaynab said, complet-
ing his thought. She rubbed her thumb over the
back of his hand, leaning in. "It's okay. I'm not
judging you. No one in their right mind would,
Ara. You were young, you just lost your parents and now you had to step up and be your
whole family to your sister. Honestly, I'd have
fallen apart."

He nearly had too. The first few years were
the worst. On top of being Anisa's primary
caregiver, juggling his schooling while sitting
in on company meetings and learning the ropes
from some of his parents' most trusted execu-
tives, it was almost too much for an eighteen-
year-old to handle.

"I didn't have time for my friends, barely had

time to myself, and so with each year I found less of a reason for Eid." And when Anisa eventually learned to stop asking him to take her to the Eid festivities happening in town, and she'd slip away with friends instead, Ara had retired from celebrating.

Until now, he thought, looking at Zaynab and acknowledging that it was her who'd given him a new outlook on the holiday.

"Today has been…illuminating. I forgot how Eid could be." At least what Eid was like when one was surrounded by the love of family, friends and community.

Ara smiled at her, the weight that had been pressing down on him mysteriously lighter now. If he hadn't known better, he'd have said she cured him.

But he realized that he'd done that on his own. *By talking to her*, he surmised. Letting out some of his most consuming thoughts and easing his burden.

He looked down at Zaynab's hand on his, knowing in his heart that she was one of the people he cared most for.

Never had Zaynab imagined that she'd have a chance to spend Eid with Ara. Certainly not with their divorce looming over their heads. Then again, she also never dreamed that she would be twenty-two weeks pregnant and counting. So she supposed life had thrown her quite a few curveballs lately.

Living with him again had been a concern, but Zaynab could now see she'd worried in vain. Ara was nothing like the cold, distant version she'd gotten of him the first time they had moved in together. Now he was spending time with her, opening up to her about himself and his past, and being vulnerable in this sweetly trusting way that had her heart and mind all twisted up with thoughts of him.

Thoughts that were heating up her body and making her want to shrug off her blazer and flap a hand over her blushing cheeks.

She'd always been physically attracted to Ara. And though that was what first hooked her when she met him, she'd stuck around because she had seen glimpses of unbridled passion lurking inside him. Not the zeal that she had seen him direct at his business, but a hunger that he starved and kept caged away deep within.

Zaynab had known it was there, and it was also ultimately why she had married him, yet she hadn't gotten to feel its full brunt until he'd kissed her and consummated their marriage for the first time.

And now, besides carrying the consequence

of that powerful ardor of his, there existed this hole in her brimming with longing.

When she wasn't tiptoeing around it, she was flat-out resisting her yearning for him.

Ara seemed clueless, and she mostly preferred it that way, except for when she wondered if he felt anything of what she was feeling.

Zaynab peeked under her lashes up at him, looking for any obvious signs that pointed to him wanting her.

They were standing on the footpath, beneath the blooming magnolia in front of their home, their car and driver having only just dropped them off. Ara's hand closed around her arm, stopping her from pushing through their front gate.

Turning very slowly to face him, and seeing how close he was to her now, she smiled nervously.

There was a charged current in the air, like a storm crackling warningly even though the sky was beautifully clear.

Her mother was staying with her and Ara, but she'd told them to head home without her and that Salma's parents, whom she'd bumped into at the festival, would be driving her home later.

Zaynab was glad for that now as Ara crowded her against the wrought iron gate, his hand moving up, long, agile fingers curling under her chin and tipping her head back. Oddly, despite the lovely early spring weather, they were alone out on the footpath. And so not a soul would have witnessed when Ara stroked his thumb along her bottom lip, his brown eyes never softer and warmer than right that instant.

"I had a good day," he said, his voice husky and low.

"Did you? I'm glad," she chirped, not knowing what else to say, his touch having apparently fried her brain.

"Thank you."

"For?" she squeaked.

"Today. For reminding me what Eid could feel like again."

She was still a little speechless, but she managed to whisper, "You're welcome," right before her brain actually shorted on her. Because Ara's thumb stilled on her lower lip as he pulled in and kissed her forehead, his warm mouth like a searing brand to remind her of this moment forever.

Zaynab hadn't even thought she'd closed her eyes until she opened them at the feel of Ara pulling back. But all he'd done was move his hand over to frame her cheek. Her disappointment didn't last too long as Ara flicked his powerful gaze to her lips, and a second later, he slowly inched his head lower. And unlike when they were at the masjid, and it seemed to her that he had intended to kiss her then, this time nothing and no one interrupted them. The only thing that stood between them was the short time it took for his mouth to seal hotly over hers.

He kissed her with that hidden hunger she'd married him for, and though she sensed he was holding back, there was nevertheless a passion in the way his lips and tongue stroked hers, and a longing from how his arms wrapped around her and hauled her against him.

She didn't think anything could pry her apart from him.

No, nothing could make her want to break away from the fierceness of his kiss.

Absolutely nothing—

Ara ripped back from her, breathing hard and touching his forehead to hers. "We shouldn't have done that. I shouldn't have…" He broke off and gnashed his teeth, drawing back from her and jerkily lowering his hands off her burning face, as though touching her had scalded him.

"I don't want to compromise your iddah, Zaynab. That kiss… *Any* intimacy would ruin it."

His rational explanation pressed pause on her humiliation. Now she understood why he was suddenly acting skittish.

"I understand," she said, still winded from their deep kiss.

"For now, let's just pretend it didn't happen."
As he said that though, the heat from earlier
crept back into his eyes.

Zaynab gazed back at him, and the butter-
flies trapped in her ribcage whirled about and
smacked into her rabbiting heart. She tried to
reconcile this man in front of her with the man
who had driven her to ask for a divorce.

The same man who her criminal father had
accused of spying on him.

She knew why she'd married Ara…

But is that why he married me? To use her
to spy on her father.

A new ache manifested in her then. This one
begging for her to ask Ara if any of that was
true. Was their marriage ever real to him at
any point?

Instead of voicing her doubt out loud, Zaynab shoved it back into the dark corner of her
mind where it had a semipermanent home and
where it couldn't interfere with this happy little moment.

CHAPTER TEN

ZAYNAB WAS SURE she could name several positives of being pregnant, but not when she was getting up every other hour to go relieve herself.

Groaning loudly, she kicked out of her bedsheets and drew up to a seat, feeling blindly for her slippers and shuffling to the ensuite.

Of course when she slipped back into bed was when her stomach chose to grumble incessantly. Knowing there was no point in trying to go back to sleep, she left her bed again and walked zombie-like to her bedroom door. At one in the morning, she expected the house to be quiet. Even though Ara had been working more these past few weeks, and sometimes well into the night, he'd be in his office on the ground floor, and so any noises he might have made wouldn't bother her where she slept on the third and topmost floor of their home.

Naturally, Zaynab tensed as what sounded

to her like a muffled moan broke the peaceful hush and froze her in her tracks.

But the hallway was empty, the wall sconces dimmed and casting shadows.

There were three other bedrooms on that floor. Two were empty, but the third one, at the front of the hall and closest to the stairs was Ara's bedroom. The door was always closed to his room, and she'd only ever been in there once since they had moved in together over three months ago. And though she wanted to respect his privacy, when she heard another faint noise coming from that vicinity, Zaynab walked slowly to his room.

As she did, two thoughts struck her. Either Ara had called it an early night, or it wasn't him at all and a burglar had broken in…

Ara wouldn't make it easy for any burglar.

Zaynab snorted softly, allaying her fears quickly. With all the measures he'd taken to safeguard the house for them, she couldn't help but feel a little bad for any thief who targeted them.

In front of his bedroom door, Zaynab hesitated and lowered the hand she had raised to knock. She didn't want to go barging in there and alarm him for no reason. Worse, he could be fast asleep, tired from all the work he was doing. Suddenly, it seemed silly to wake him simply because she'd heard a strange noise or two, especially since she now noticed whatever it was had stopped making the sound.

Just as she began chalking it up to her sleep-addled brain hallucinating the whole thing, Zaynab stilled as the noise rose up again. She pressed her ear to Ara's door, and holding her breath, she listened.

There! Another moan—or maybe it was a groan?—pressured her into deciding.

That's it. I'm going in there.

Because naked or not, his well-being was important to her. She wouldn't ever forgive herself if he had injured himself and she didn't check to see whether he needed help.

Grasping his door handle, Zaynab knew the door would open. He'd once told her that she could come fetch him at any time during the night if she required him. But right then it was Ara who needed her, and so she was relieved that he'd had the forethought of leaving his bedroom unlocked.

She squinted into the darkness, waiting for her eyes to adjust a little before she treaded inside.

The moaning was much louder now that she was in the room with him. Without the door muffling the noise, she could make out the distressed notes in his groans.

"Ara?" she called out softly. Emboldened by her own bravery as she crept closer to the bed, she raised her voice. "Ara? Wake up. You're having a bad dream."

At least that was what she supposed was happening.

She could see his shadowy form in the bed and moved closer, trying to see if he was facing her direction or not. Resisting the urge to turn back and flick on the bedroom lights, she gripped the edge of the bed, leaned in and called his name once more.

He grunted in answer and shifted in his sleep.

"Ara—" Zaynab's breath hitched when he suddenly flopped onto his back, his hand fisting his sheets, and even though she couldn't see his face, she could hear the contorted pain in his rasping breaths. Whatever demons were chasing him in his dreams, they appeared to be catching up and fast.

She didn't know what made her do it, but she reached out and touched his hand, caressing the tension from his knuckles.

It seemed to be working. In his sleep, Ara relaxed, his hand loosening over the bedsheets and his breathing evening out. She smiled, happy to have brought him some comfort. And for a while she was content to stand guard and protect him from the worst of his terrors.

But once Zaynab thought to slip away and let him get some rest, he turned his hand around and caught her wrist, startling her into almost screaming out.

When her heart rate returned to normal, she tried to gently pull away, and when that didn't work, she attempted to pry his fingers off her wrist.

About to just pinch the back of his hand and wake him when he started murmuring, she stopped trying to break free and listened as the incoherent mumbling turned into words.

"Stop… Don't… Not them… Hooyo… No, *no*, don't… No, aabo…"

Realizing he was dreaming of his parents gave the nightmare context. Zaynab went still, the fight to force his hand off her arm no longer a priority, and her heart twisting in her chest for him, knowing she could never rescue him from the terror of his past. Ara's hand squeezed tighter, his grasp moving into bone-crushing territory very quickly.

"Ara!" she cried out and slapped the back of his hand before digging in her nails and hoping that did the trick.

"Zaynab?"

Hearing him say her name in confusion didn't let up the pain he was unknowingly inflicting on her.

"You're crushing my hand!" she yelped through gritted teeth.

Immediately, his fingers went lax over her wrist in response. Slipping out of his hold and clutching her throbbing hand to her chest, she saw him move in the dark, his bulkier shadow shifting over to the side a few seconds before the room was bathed in soft, white light.

She blinked rapidly, wishing he'd have warned her first.

Once her eyes adjusted to the change in lighting, she saw him leaning back against his headboard, shirtless, the remote controlling his room lights in his hands and a darkly questioning look lasered on her.

"What are you doing?"

"You were having a nightmare. I just came in to check on you, and then you started squeezing my hand really hard." She winced as she prodded her wrist, sensing a bruise in her near future. "Remind me not to try waking you again," she muttered, blushing and looking away when his piercing stare bored into her. Then in the silence, she shuffled a couple steps back to the open bedroom door, wondering if she could make a smooth exit.

Before she could try, Ara drew off his bedclothes in a flourish, revealing that he hadn't been sleeping in the nude.

Still his black silk pajama bottoms left little to the imagination. And hers was happily spinning out fantasies as he closed the distance to her in a few long strides.

He held out his hand to her.

Understanding what he wanted, Zaynab slowly pulled out her arm to him and allowed Ara to take her hand.

"Easy," she said with a grimace as his fingers gently brushed over the now tender underside of her wrist.

She had been annoyed with him until she saw his brows furrow and his lips thin in what looked to her to be a mix of regret and concern. And she certainly heard it smacking in his low tone as he observed, "I've hurt you."

"No, I'm fine, really. I just bruise easily is all."

"We have to ice this now," Ara said, not having shifted the blame off himself and taking immediate action to remedy his mistake.

"Hold the ice there, and I'll just grab the ointment."

After leaving her with those instructions, Ara moved fast to the cloakroom, grabbed the first aid kit and headed back to where Zaynab was waiting for him in the kitchen.

Glad to see that she was listening and holding

the ice pack to her wound, he moved to stand beside her rather than take the other stool at the kitchen peninsula. He didn't deserve comfort, not after what he'd done to her. Even before she'd revealed her unhappiness and asked for a divorce, Ara had suspected he could hurt her, but he never thought that threat to her could be physical.

But as he took a deep breath, and gently pulled the towel-wrapped ice pack off her hand, he came face-to-face with the pain he caused her.

Reddened flesh ringed her wrist and glared up at Ara accusingly.

I did that to her...

He forced his hands from clenching into fists, keeping them steady while he opened the first aid kit and pulled out the anti-inflammatory salve he needed from it.

"I can do that," Zaynab offered.

But he shook his head and lied, "It will be a lot quicker if I do it."

She gave him a look that said she didn't believe that for one bit. The truth was that he needed to atone for his mistake, and it would be easier for them both if she would let him have his way. Expecting Zaynab to argue, he was surprised when she simply slid her injured hand closer to him and waited patiently.

Though she was compliant, sitting through his swabbing the salve onto a cotton bud and massaging it lightly over the red imprints of his fingers on her, she asked, "I understand the ice pack, but isn't the ointment a little excessive?"

"The ice will keep the swelling from spreading, and the ointment with any inflammation."

"It's a bruise. I've had plenty and they usually mend themselves," she said before smiling and cocking her head to the side. "More importantly, where did you learn to be such a good nurse?"

"You'll have to thank Anisa. She was running around all the time and hurting herself as a kid." He rested her hand down on the towel and ice pack, capping the ointment and tossing the used cotton bud in the dustbin.

"Bumps, cuts, scrapes and loads of bruises. She even broke her arm once, and since I couldn't repair the fracture myself, we had to make a hospital trip."

Zaynab laughed. "Sounds like a typical enough childhood."

He supposed it was, but after losing their mother and father so suddenly and violently, Ara hadn't wanted Anisa to leave him too. Although as her older brother he'd always been fiercely protective of her, when half their family was gone overnight, his overprotectiveness of Anisa had only intensified multiple times over. When she was younger she hadn't minded it as much, clinging to him more in the absence of their parents. But as she grew older, Anisa would rebuff his helicoptering, until she finally told him she was moving abroad for her post-secondary studies and career.

"I might have cared for her a little too much," he admitted gruffly.

"You were her older brother. From what I've heard Salma tell me, it comes with the territory."

Ara wished he could take Zaynab's comfort, but he said, "I didn't approve of her leaving to study and work abroad, and so in my anger, I stopped talking to her and we didn't speak for four years."

Four long years that he'd wasted being angry with her. That was time he could never get back, but that he was trying to repair, starting by helping her with her upcoming wedding.

"I'm sure she's only happy that you're speaking again." Zaynab echoed what he hoped: that Anisa didn't hold a grudge against him for how childishly he'd acted.

Talking about his sister was reminding him of his parents and the nightmare he'd just had of them. If he closed his eyes and listened carefully, he swore the explosions of bombs reverberated in his mind, the screams for help from the injured, his mother's wails and his father's cries for help all mingling together into blaring white noise—

"Ara?" Zaynab was leaning forward, her fingertips touching his over the cool marble counter. "You looked deep in thought there."

He frowned when she pulled her touch away, relying on the calm she brought him. Grateful that she stopped the nightmare from pushing into his reality, and clinging onto the distraction she presented, he asked, "Why are you awake so late anyway?"

"Well, first, I needed to go to the washroom," she said while a shyness tinged her smile, "and then I was too hungry to go back to sleep."

Realizing that he could help her there, Ara headed for the fridge. "Let me fix you something."

"No need! I was craving pickles again."

Standing before the open fridge doors, he smiled despite the dark mood still clinging to him. He grabbed the pickles she requested and two plates and forks.

He wasn't smiling though when, spearing a pickle, Zaynab glanced at him and wondered, "So, what were you dreaming about? It sounded terrifying."

"It was," he agreed.

"Maybe you'd feel better if you talked about it."

Ara highly doubted that it would do him any good, and he was opening his mouth to tell her that, only Zaynab then said, "In your sleep, you called to your mother and father. That's why I thought, perhaps, you would want to talk about it."

Hearing that he'd been crying out for them poured ice through his veins. He didn't know what made him colder, that Zaynab knew it was his parents he'd dreamed of, or that he was opening his mouth to explain.

"I was dreaming of them."

"Does that happen often?"

Shaking his head, his thoughts all jumbled, he answered, "No. Not anymore. But, at first, yes." Sighing, he tried again and with the hope he sounded more articulate. "The dreams were worse right after their deaths."

"Have you tried talking to someone?"

She meant a therapist. As much as there were things he loved about Somalia and Somaliland, the progress toward mental health was still slow going there, the stigma and superstition far stronger around it than in the UK.

"No, I haven't seen a professional. Though I imagine it could help, I've mostly outgrown the terrors."

Zaynab's frown told him she thought otherwise, but she wisely didn't push the subject, not when he was barely getting through their conversation.

"My work in Mogadishu must have me thinking of them more lately. They always wanted to expand their business there.

"Truthfully," he rasped, "I don't know why I'm dreaming of them."

Sometimes he wondered if it was because he would soon be a parent himself. A part of him did worry that he wouldn't know what to do when it came time for him to hold his and Zaynab's baby in his arms. That he wouldn't be able to protect his family this time either, and that, just as he hadn't been there to save his mother and father from their cold-hearted killers and lost them forever, he'd lose Zaynab and their child too.

She didn't know that his parents had been murdered.

Ara had kept that fact hidden from not just Zaynab, but most people. It was an ugly but crucial detail that was left out of all of the media reports. A boating accident was the tragic story spun for the public, and he'd been happy to go along with it if it kept people from interfering with his grief.

But now, and most illogically, he wanted to tell her of all people.

So, he did.

"When I dream of them, they're always crying out to me, begging me to help them just before they sink under the ocean and drown." Ara's breaths sawed out faster, his heart pounding against his sternum. "But just now, in this dream, they were trapped under a building rocked by an explosion." It wasn't unlike what had happened to him in Mogadishu. If he hadn't been found by a group of volunteers searching the smoking rubble of the hotel that had been targeted, Ara accepted that he would've died that day.

He didn't know why his dream had diverged this one time. His only theory was that his brain had merged the two tragedies together, and in doing so, amplified the terror of both and tortured him.

"Like I said, I don't know why exactly it's happening now. But then again, I could be having the dreams because they were killed." He said it so casually, forcibly detaching himself from the powerful emotions violently churning inside of him. They wouldn't sink him under, not with the way Zaynab's eyes widened and she slid off her stool and approached him slowly.

Ara could see what she wanted to ask, so he said, "I didn't say anything because most people don't know it's the truth. And because their killers are long gone and will likely never be punished for their crime."

"Ara, I'm… I can't even…"

"It's fine," he said stiffly, excusing her from struggling to find words and turning away from the pity he worried was coming. He expected the awkward quiet that came with his confession.

What he wasn't ready for was Zaynab's arms to slip around his middle.

She hugged him from the side, her cheek pressed up against his shoulder and her eyes closed, a sniffle drifting up to his ears. It wasn't long after that he felt her tears wetting the T-shirt he'd tossed on before coming down to the kitchen with her.

He was stunned, and not only because of her embrace but that she was crying for him.

Tears that he hadn't allowed himself to cry.

And now with her soft, breathy sobs the only sound between them, Ara felt a strange heat burning his eyes and clawing at his throat. It would be a first, as he hadn't even cried when he'd laid his parents to rest. No, even then he had to hold strong for his sister and their family's business.

But he knew that if he let go of the part that held him from leaning into the warm support she offered, and if he hugged Zaynab back, that

Ara would do what he'd always fought against doing…

I'll fall apart, he thought with gritted teeth and tears filling up his eyes fast, knowing that he wouldn't be able to stop if that ever happened.

Afraid of the feelings she'd unlocked in him, Ara pulled away from her and cleared his throat of the hoarseness clogging it, his gaze purposefully avoiding hers.

"If you're done eating, you should head back upstairs and try to sleep… For the baby." He added the last part, hoping that she didn't think he was trying to control her.

When she didn't respond, he hazarded a glance at her and regretted it instantly. She was gazing at him with redness tinging her eyes, her lashes darkly wet from her tears and her chin trembling as though she was fighting to hold back a fresh display of waterworks on his behalf. Wildly, none of it robbed her of her beauty.

And all that observation made him want to do was bundle her up in his arms and hold her for as long as they both needed.

"You should come up and sleep too," she implored.

She was right. He should try and sleep, but with everything he'd experienced—the nightmare of his parents, bruising Zaynab accidentally, then revealing to her that his mother and father were murdered and making her cry—Ara didn't think he'd be resting peacefully anytime soon.

"Maybe," he said noncommittally, "but I'll be in my office until then, if you require me."

He sensed her lingering, hopeful look fixed on him for a while, but eventually Zaynab gave up. And it was only when she was slowly walking away from him that Ara looked longingly after her.

CHAPTER ELEVEN

ZAYNAB LIKED TO think of herself as being quite patient.

At least she *had* a lot of patience, but the next few days following her and Ara's late-night tête-à-tête featuring her craving for pickles and his nightmares had shown her that she couldn't wait around for him to make the first move. Not unless she wasn't willing for the awkward silence between them to ever get better again and go back to the way it was before it began feeling like he was drifting away from her intentionally.

And she had the sense it was purposeful. Like Ara was erecting the same unclimbable barriers at the start of their marriage, when they were first living with each other. Laying those bricks down, piece by piece, and concealing the secret parts of himself that he'd been showing her slowly but steadily since they'd moved back in together.

It was those hidden parts to him that she recognized had been the reason she'd fallen for him in the first place.

His honest thoughts and feelings, and his unbridled passion; all of it back behind those tall, thorny walls around him. That haunted her the most. All that progress... *Only for him to return to the way he was*. To the man that she'd wanted to divorce.

Zaynab had mulled over it for several days now. She'd already been quietly worrying about his work schedule creeping into the time that he used to spend with her. But she hadn't said anything, figuring that he wouldn't be preoccupied with his business affairs forever. And she knew that his work was important to him, and she wanted to support him because of it. If that meant that she stood by quietly and kept her unease to herself, then so be it.

But she questioned whether staying quiet was the right choice, or if she'd only been ignoring the warning signs dropping like breadcrumbs and pointing toward the frustrating changes in Ara. Now Zaynab was staring longingly outside his office door, her hand poised to knock but her courage wavering on her at the very last moment.

She was still undecided whether to go in when the double doors suddenly swung open, forcing her to startle back and stare wide-eyed at Ara as he stepped aside with a silent invitation for her to enter.

This wasn't the first time she had entered his workspace. Naturally well-lit by an array of long, narrow picture windows, anyone walking in would immediately be drawn to the focal point of the space: a massive L-shaped executive desk that oozed luxury with its gleaming dark-stained wood surface, supple leather inlaid desktop and modesty panel, and exquisite craftsmanship that gave the desk its illusion of floating from where she stood at the office's entrance. The other furnishings were two high back leather accent armchairs, a glass coffee table and a credenza doubling as a coffee station.

The only difference in his office was that Ara wasn't alone.

A young black man was standing in the corner with a tablet grasped in his hands and a smile directed at her.

He looked familiar, though she couldn't place him in her memory right then, and she was more curious how Ara had known she was outside.

"How did you know I was…" She trailed off, seeing exactly how he'd known that she was skulking outside his office doors.

Framed by built-in shelves, a large flat screen showcased several tinier monitors, twelve in total, and she immediately recognized they were locations through the house from the kitchen to the staircase, the front hall, and dining and sitting rooms and right outside their front and back property.

Ara had told her about the security measures, and though he'd pointed out the hidden cameras, it had never occurred to her to ask him to see the feeds.

But she now knew how he had detected her presence and known to open his office doors for her.

And at the same time it struck Zaynab that he must have seen her standing outside nervously.

Before she could slink off in embarrassment, Ara asked, "Is there something you needed, Zaynab?" and, with a jolt, reminded her why she had come seeking him in the first place.

"I thought we could have lunch together?" Zaynab eyed the familiar man whose face she still couldn't place, adding softly, "Unless you're busy."

"We were just about to take a break," the smiling man chimed in.

Ara's scowl said otherwise, but he nodded and his features appeared to soften the longer he regarded her.

"Let's reconvene in an hour or so." Ara inclined his head at the man before he turned the full power of his gaze on her. "Did you have any-place in mind for our lunch?"

"Who was that man back in your office?" Zaynab asked as soon as the server left them with their lunch orders.

They were seated out in the open at her request, and though the security risk would've been lower inside the café, Ara had to admit that she was right about it being too beautiful a day to waste sitting indoors. That and there was a calming effect to watching people go about their lives on the popular, shop-lined street. Couple the pleasantly balmy spring weather with the rare sunshine beaming overhead, and it only seemed to lure more people than usual outdoors.

"Daniel. He works for the security company I've hired."

"I knew he looked familiar! And Daniel works for your sister's fiancé, Nasser, right?"

"That's correct." He'd been working with Daniel for a while now, and as the head of his security team Daniel had earned Ara's trust in shaping the safety measures around his business and also around the home and life he shared with Zaynab. But these days, he barely saw and spoke to her.

It was torturous to yearn so desperately to be

with her, but to also know that it was safer for him to avoid her.

Because he was starting to give away too many of his secrets to her. Telling her about the real cause of his parents' deaths had made that obvious to him.

It's safer for her too.

He'd physically harmed her by bruising her during one of his night terrors. Then made her cry when she had learned about his parents' murder. And, if all that wasn't enough, Ara couldn't allow himself to forget that their divorce was still very real and possibly on the horizon as her delivery date quickly approached.

In a couple months, their six-month arrangement to live under one roof would come to an end. Zaynab would have to decide, once and for all, if a divorce was what she desired.

And though a part of him still wanted her to choose to stay with him, a new feeling began to stir inside of him, driving in deeper the wedge that had appeared between them over these past weeks, and this emergent emotion was pushing him toward letting her go.

Freeing her from any obligation to him.

Though he hadn't been willing to listen, it was as she said once: they never needed to be married to co-parent. *I just wasn't ready to let her leave yet*, he quietly admitted, if only to himself.

The sullen mood at their table was at odds with the bright, sunshine-filled day.

Head bowed and eyes glued to her plate, Zaynab was eating, but her heart didn't seem into it.

Feeling like a monster, he opened his mouth to apologize for his far from stellar company and was interrupted by his phone lighting up. He had set it on mute, but he left it facing up on the table by his plate, in case anything came up that required his urgent response. And seeing his little sister's name flash on his phone screen activated his brotherly worry for her.

"Anisa, what's the matter?"

Ara yanked the phone away from his ear at Anisa's sudden shriek, the sound more excited than terrified, but hearing it still ratcheted his heart rate through the roof.

"Happy birthday to you!" she sang loudly and out of tune.

Zaynab must have heard his sister's off-key singing because her curiosity flashed into surprise.

After her singing, Anisa chattered away and asked him about how he was spending his birthday.

Considering he'd completely forgotten what day it was, he grumbled, "I'm working."

Anisa sighed as loudly in his ears as she'd sung, then lectured him about needing to lighten his workload before finally revealing the reason she had called.

"Nasser and I are coming for a visit." She went on to explain that it was to do some shopping for her wedding later on that year—shopping she could have easily done where she was now in Canada. Which was why he sensed that the visit was also a good excuse for her to check in on him. Anisa had been texting him regularly since he'd come to London. She knew that he was living with Zaynab and that she was pregnant, and as excited as she was to be an aunt soon, he felt an undercurrent of worry from her. Though he didn't know if it was worry for him or Zaynab, or heck, even the baby, whatever Anisa's real reason for the sudden visit, he would always still welcome her.

So, instead of interrogating her, he asked, "When?"

"Four days from today. I know it's short notice, but we've already booked our flight."

Ara let her know that was fine, and after exchanging a few more pleasantries, they ended their call. He placed his phone down and acknowledged Zaynab's inquisitive look.

"My sister and Nasser are coming for a visit. She was also calling because… Well, I'm sure you heard her."

"I think half the café and street did," she remarked dryly on Anisa's screeching over his birthday, earning a small, amused smile from him.

"Anisa's always been *expressive*."

Zaynab laughed breezily. "Well, it will be nice to finally meet her. And, even better, they'll be here for the baby shower next week." Then after a noticeable pause, and looking far more solemn, she said, "I didn't know it was your birthday."

He stopped smiling and shrugged, knowing that her intrigue was warranted.

"It might sound like a lie, but I forgot what day it was." In the same way he hadn't celebrated Eid for years before this recent one with Zaynab, his birthday had become a nonevent since his parents' passing. Another reminder of a personal life event that was stolen from him with their deaths. "Anisa might be the only one who remembers what day it is," he said. And even then, for the four years he and his sister hadn't spoken, he'd gone without any birthday wishes.

Zaynab sat in contemplative silence, but then she smiled and said, "Happy birthday. I guess lunch is on me then."

Though he tried to argue, when the bill came and the server held out a payment terminal, Zaynab tapped her card faster than he could.

Ara couldn't find it in himself to be annoyed, not with the way her triumphant grin made him smile. And she continued to smile even after his phone interrupted them again, the screen lighting up with Daniel's name this time.

"We're on our way," he said after seeing that nearly two hours had elapsed since he and Zaynab had left the house for their lunch. He rang up the driver next. Even though they had walked the fifteen minutes to the café, it was time he didn't want to lose walking back now.

"Actually, I'm going to stay behind and meet up with Salma soon anyway. She wants to do a little shopping."

Hearing the first of this, Ara frowned but nodded. He didn't like leaving her, but her friend would be keeping her company soon. "All right, but you have the driver's number. Call him when you're done shopping. I'll even let him know to give Salma a ride if she wishes it."

Zaynab thanked him, and in a few minutes, he was in the back of the car and pulling away from where she sat alone at their table, watching and waving to him.

Despite having a criminal for a father, deception and guile didn't come as naturally to Zaynab.

So lying to Ara about Salma meeting with her and sending him off back to the work that lately consumed his attention was hard on her. But the moment the car ferrying him away turned the corner, she sprang up and strode away from the café, determination setting her shoulders straight and holding her head up high.

She was on a secret mission to make this birthday as special for him as possible.

But as she walked into the cute, colorful little shops lined along Notting Hill's famous Portobello Road, Zaynab found this was a far easier task imagined than accomplished.

She had gotten to know more about Ara since living with him here in London then when she'd first married him and moved into his beautiful big home in Berbera. And yet shopping for the man was still a challenge. He seemed to have everything at his fingertips already, what with his tremendous fortune. What could he possibly want that she alone could give him?

Still, Zaynab managed to cobble together what she thought might work, and after shopping for a couple hours, she took up his offer and rang for the driver.

She swore the driver to secrecy as he helped haul her shopping bags into the car, and then from the car and inside the house. Giving him a tip and thanking him, Zaynab sneaked upstairs, praying that none of Ara's security cameras caught and ruined her surprise for him.

She'd tried her best to disguise the presents with innocuous brown paper bags. He would only think she'd been shopping a lot, and that would keep him from guessing what she had in store.

Once alone in her room, Zaynab set to work wrapping his birthday gifts.

Her back ached by the time she sat back and admired her hard but loving effort to surprise him.

Now she wasn't deluding herself into thinking that her presents would, like magic, fix whatever had frayed between them. But she did hope that it would be a start to a conversation toward healing and that this hurdle before them would be only that, an obstacle they could surmount together.

With that positive mindset buoying her spirit, Zaynab went about her day as normally as possible and counted out the hours until dinner when she would see him next.

In spite of his workload, Ara still ate meals with her regularly enough. Yet the mood between them was decidedly different than what it used to be. Rather than the easy flowing conversation, he now spoke less frequently and getting him to talk more than a few words was like squeezing blood from a stone. She might as well be chatting with herself sometimes…

Or better yet, a wall.

Zaynab sighed, shaking off the sourness crowding in with her despairing thoughts and smiling until she felt hopeful again.

Because there was no way Ara wouldn't be knocked off his feet with this surprise. When the familiar decadent smells of a warm freshly cooked meal perfumed the entire house, Zaynab crept out of her room with the gift bag behind her back and hurried faster downstairs than she usually did.

Though he'd been working more, he still found time to cook for her. And just as every evening before, Ara had the table set and ready when she entered the dining room, and all she had to do was grab the seat beside him at the far end of the table.

He was already seated and waiting on her.

Normally they would eat, but Zaynab didn't sit immediately, instead standing by her chair and attempting to not squirm or fidget when Ara looked up at her raptly.

Blushing plenty though, she cleared her throat and pulled around the gift bag she hid behind her back. "For you," she said quickly and almost breathlessly.

She had a whole pretty speech prepared, but she forgot all of it the instant his eyes clapped on her.

He didn't keep her waiting, taking the silver

straps of the gift bag and pushing away his table setting to open his present.

One by one, he silently pulled out the gifts. A self-heating mug for all the tea he drank, a silly book full of dad jokes that he could use when their baby was older and a photo album he opened to the first page and where she'd tucked into the photo sleeve the first and more recently second ultrasound of Button, side by side.

Zaynab sucked in her lips, the gifts self-explanatory, but still wanting to explain what each gift meant to her and, hopefully, what it could mean to him.

Eventually Ara stood and walked up to her.

She held perfectly still, waiting to see what he would do and finally hoping to understand how he felt.

"Thank you," he said simply, his voice deeper and gruffer with indiscernible emotion. Even now his eyes were guarded and his expression closed off to her.

But when he took hold of her shoulders, Zaynab's rising concern eased off. He kissed her forehead, the imprint of when he'd done it first at Eid still emblazoned in her mind and heart. She expected it to feel the same but it didn't. Desperate to recreate that feeling from before, she closed her eyes and leaned in, her nose tickled by his beard and her rounder, tauter baby bump pressed up against the hard, flat planes of his abs beneath his soft dress shirt.

She only opened her eyes when he lifted his mouth away and held her back at arm's length.

Looking at him was torture afterward, seeing the emptiness staring back at her when her lungs were constricted so tightly it hurt to breathe. Hurt to speak up as he sat back down, returned her gifts into the larger gift bag and placed it aside at the foot of the dining table like all of it was an afterthought now to whatever came next. In this case, their dinner. And then later, she knew, it would be his work that took precedence over everything else. Including being with her.

And although Ara had shown his gratitude, it had felt empty. *Forced*, she observed sadly.

Not knowing what to say, and disappointed by his lackluster reaction, Zaynab compelled herself to take her seat when all she wanted to do was run upstairs to the refuge of her bedroom, where she could cry the heartbroken tears she was holding back right then.

CHAPTER TWELVE

ONCE AGAIN ARA was destroying a good thing he had going with Zaynab.

He'd already ruined his marriage, and now he was demolishing the good impression that he had worked hard to achieve in the short time they had lived together once more. And even though he knew his actions were hurting her, and he wanted to stop, apologize and grovel his way back into her good graces, Ara just couldn't bring himself to do it.

Like a train careening fast toward a break in the tracks, all he had to look forward to was the promise of a steep plunge and the fiery wreck awaiting him in the end.

And the end appeared to be the baby shower Salma offered to host on his and Zaynab's behalf.

"Here are the parents-to-be!" Salma announced their arrival to the guests now all gathered in the spacious and well-tended back garden and patio of her parents' home.

Having arrived for their visit a couple days ago, Anisa and Nasser were the only guests on his side. And aside from her mother, who Ara had flown in for the party, everyone else who came up to congratulate them were friends of Zaynab's.

He recognized her friend Neelima from the restaurant, and then there was her octogenarian client, Opaline. With Opaline was the man who'd been in Zaynab's resort suite in Mauritius, and whom Ara now knew after researching was Opaline's grandnephew, Remi. Though he had no right to it, certainly not after how he'd been acting toward Zaynab as of late, Ara still tensed up when Remi's friendly smile shined down over her and his hand touched her arm, lingering there as he passed his well wishes on her soon-to-be motherhood.

Zaynab smiled back at Remi, looking far more relaxed in that one moment than she had with Ara in a long while. Not since he'd been slowly retreating from her and the warmth and happiness she made him desire so very badly. Happiness that he frankly felt no right to, not when he was so confident that he'd end up hurting her.

I've hurt her before, haven't I?

He had pushed her to the point of divorcing him. It had to have been a last resort for her.

Knowing Zaynab, she wouldn't have married him at all if she'd thought it would end in the dissolution of their marriage a year later.

No, Ara thought. He'd forced her hand with his cold attitude, and he was doing it again now.

"Are you all right?" Zaynab quietly asked him at one point as they were taking pictures beneath a white trellis wrapped by pretty, vibrantly bright flowering vines. She was alternating between looking at him and the phone cameras guests were holding up at them, smiling for everybody else, but the light of the gesture didn't truly reach her dark eyes as she peered up at him. "Because if you're not, you can tell me."

"I'm fine," he gritted out the lie.

Zaynab's glare could have frosted the blooming flowers above their heads. "Really?" she said, her voice low, her words only for his ears. "You could've fooled me. It looks like you'd rather be anywhere else."

"Zaynab…"

She narrowed her eyes at him as though quietly warning him off telling her any more falsehoods.

With possibly the worst timing, the professional photographer Salma had hired for the baby shower instructed, "That's a good pose! Get in a little closer and just hold it there for a few seconds, please."

Ara froze as Zaynab turned into him, smoothed her hands over the lapels of his suit jacket and gazed up at him, heeding the photographer's instructions to the letter. To everyone else they must have appeared like an adoring couple eternally in love. She might have even fooled him if he wasn't chilled by the emptiness looking up at him now. Like she'd utterly given up on trying to reach him, and somehow, that thought withered his already low opinion of himself.

"Perfect," the photographer called out, aiming their lens at the other guests in attendance and giving them a break.

Zaynab quickly removed her hands from him and turned to walk away. He took a step after her instinctively but faltered in the follow-through and let her go in the end.

She didn't look back at him once as she mingled with the guests, smiling warmly at everyone but him. Zaynab strolled through the garden in her beautiful pink dress and warmly welcomed the people who had taken precious time out of their day to celebrate with them. He should have been by her side doing the exact same thing, but instead, he stood apart from the party and general merriment, and merely spectated the festive mood all around him.

He could have been admiring the lengths that

Salma had gone to in making this party a beautiful affair.

Gold and white balloons and streamers festooned the wooden fence cordoning off the backyard and the sliding glass doors into Salma's parents' home. Upbeat pop music played from someone's portable Bluetooth speaker, and a catered buffet spread was ready to be enjoyed on two long folding tables. It was all very thoughtful of Salma to prepare for him and Zaynab, and given all the tireless effort that went to making this party happen, Ara only felt more villainous for not enjoying it as fully as he ought to have.

As he watched Zaynab from the sidelines, Ara was transported back to when he'd met her for the very first time.

He had walked up behind her as she looked out over the Indian Ocean from the bow of his yacht, the golden ribbons of sunset mirroring off the blackening waters holding his ship afloat. Sensing him before he announced his presence, Zaynab had turned slowly and, with a shy smile, she'd immediately captivated him.

She was weaving that same magic now on the party guests, her smile just as entrancing today as it was that day on his yacht.

Ara could envision her hosting his business dinners, welcoming potential new investors and helping him seal many lucrative deals for his company. Beyond that, he had selfishly wanted that smile of hers in his life forever. It was why he'd desired her from the start. Why he had chosen to make her his wife.

And why I'm in love with her.

At least to himself, Ara had never denied his strong affection for her, but it was becoming clearer to him more every day that his attraction now felt more like infatuation. He loved Zaynab, always had, and it was why he was working so hard now to keep her from getting any closer. Discourage her from loving him back. Protect her from the pain he knew he'd cause her.

Because love did that.

He'd loved his parents, and they had been killed and taken away from him. He had even deeply cared for her father before Sharmarke had been revealed to be a monster. No matter how alluring it was, loving her could only lead to his suffering. Maybe not today... *But someday.*

A muscle in his cheek hardened when Zaynab was by his side again to open the presents their guests gifted them.

She tried to avoid his eyes, but he could see that the enthusiasm she presented to her friends and mother was not as wholehearted as it might have been, and that was wholly his fault. She deserved to be happy, on this day especially. The only thing that comforted Ara right then was the knowledge that he was doing this for the good of his family. For Zaynab and their baby.

If that was the closest he could do to loving her outright then so be it.

Like any first-time expectant mother at her baby shower, Zaynab would've thought the occasion would have been a happy one. Instead, she had spent the few hours impatiently and guiltily waiting for the party to end.

And it was all because of Ara.

For over a month now she had been aware that he was acting more like the colder version of himself that she'd gotten after they first married. She'd made excuses for him quietly. *He's busy working. He just wants to help people. He'll go back to giving our relationship priority soon enough.*

But those excuses were slowly unveiling themselves to be threadbare reasons for her to overlook his off-putting and distancing attitude. And that was her mistake for not nipping it in the bud as soon as it became apparent to her. If she had, Zaynab wouldn't have had to sit through his embarrassing glacial impression in front of all the family and friends who had showed up with gifts and well wishes for their baby shower.

It would've been fine if she was alone in noticing how he was acting. Sadly, she'd had to endure several guests coming up to her and asking whether Ara was feeling all right.

She told them all the same made-up story, that he was feeling a little under the weather and that was why he appeared sullen. Since no one caught her on the barefaced lie, Zaynab assumed that Ara hadn't revealed it to be so. Unfortunately for him she couldn't find it in her heart to be thankful to him for not outing her deception as she wouldn't have been placed in that awkward position in the first place had he not forced her hand.

And had he not made her fight back from biting his head off multiple times during the party.

Managing to hold her frazzled emotions together until they were in the privacy of his vehicle was the hardest thing Zaynab had done in a long while. It was almost as difficult for her as when she'd gone to ask him for a divorce at his sister's engagement party.

Sometimes she'd questioned whether she should have gone in person all those months ago. If she had just called him to ask for the divorce instead, then they wouldn't have ever ended up in her hotel room…

And I wouldn't be pregnant.

She would never regret having their baby now, but then it wouldn't have led Ara to talking her into living together, and by that logic they wouldn't be here now, sharing the back seat of the chauffeured car with an oppressive tension settled between them.

Zaynab was just grateful now that her mother had chosen to stay behind and help Salma and her family with the party cleanup. And she was just as relieved when Anisa and Nasser had said that they were going to explore the city after the party and would find their own way home later.

With their houseguests all preoccupied, she and Ara would have the house to themselves to argue if it came to that. And she sensed that it *would* come to that. Though the luxury car had a privacy screen that would make it impossible for the driver to hear their conversation, Zaynab had hoped to wait until they were home alone together before she broached the subject of how he'd acted at the baby shower. But almost as soon as they were on the road her frustration and anger bubbled to the surface and spilled out.

"You humiliated me," she said, refusing to look at him and staring out her window instead. Not that she was paying any mind to the buildings and streets they passed on their short journey home. She just didn't want to see anything on his face that might make her stop. This was something Zaynab had to do. She had to let him know how awful he was making her feel lately. It still didn't make it easier to spit out the bitter words that felt and tasted like gravel in her mouth. "Almost everyone asked me if you weren't feeling well, and I said 'yes.' I lied to them *for you*."

Ara's long drawn-out, deep sigh snapped her head around to him, her anger blistering hot and choking her up.

"They're my friends and family, and they just hosted a party for us and our baby! Doesn't that mean anything to you?"

"Of course it does," he said calmly but his cool tone only incensed her more. "I appreci-ate—"

Zaynab scoffed, not caring that she interrupted him. Leaning in closer over the console between them in the back seat, she glared incredulously at him. Because surely he wasn't trying to argue that he hadn't been abjectly rude at the party. "Did you, really? Because your actions said otherwise. My God, Ara, you were sulking. *Sulking!* At our baby shower!" She shook her head, the rage fading as quickly as it surged, heartache and disappointment taking over. "How could you?" she accused him softly.

Then, unable to stare at him a second more without crying, Zaynab looked away, bit her trembling lower lip and fought the tears pinching the corners of her eyes. Sobbing in front of him would only undermine the point she was trying to get him to see; that he was acting terribly, and that if Ara didn't change back to the kind, sweet, thoughtfully attentive version of himself she'd seen of him, then they might not last the two months left of their six-month arrangement.

That she would have no choice but to continue with their divorce and break their family up.

As she discreetly wiped at a tear that leaked free, Zaynab was glad that Ara had read her body language perfectly and didn't attempt to reengage her in their unfinished conversation. Because they would still definitely need to talk. She only needed a moment to gain her composure again and iron out the weepiness that gripped her now. Using the rest of the car ride to do just that, Zaynab didn't speak again until they were walking through the front door of their home.

"Zaynab, I'm… I'm sorry."

Ara's apology drifted from behind her as she stormed toward the sitting room. It was spacious enough for her to pace angrily while they hashed this out.

Sensing that he followed her, Zaynab scowled and finally looked at him, her heart racing and her chest heaving.

"What are you apologizing for exactly?"

Ara's brows slammed down in consternation. "For the way I acted…" he said slowly as though testing the waters with her, and when she didn't snap his head off, he continued, "If I offended you, your mother and friends in any way, I am sorry for that. It wasn't my intention."

"Wasn't it though?" When he didn't answer, she gave her head a vigorous shake, an embittered laugh tumbling out. "I don't know what's worse—the fact that you've been acting so standoffish lately, or the lie."

"Lie?" he echoed, his eyes growing as hard and cold as hers had to be.

"Yes, your lie. I ask if you're fine, and you keep telling me that you are, but that's a lie."

She tried not to balk when he slid a step closer to her, bearing down as he gritted out, "That's not a lie."

"It is!" she retorted.

Taking another step, and then another, and backing her into the coffee table, Ara stopped his advance and glared at her. "Fine. You're

right. I wasn't the consummate guest of honor.
I just…"

"You just didn't want to be there," she said,
punching her chin up and meeting his glare fear-
lessly. She wouldn't be intimidated or guilted
into silence.

Not that she believed that was what he was
doing. Ara had never made her fear him physically, not once. The only risk he truly posed was
to her fragile emotions. *To my heart*, she thought
bitterly. And that was because she loved him.

I do love him.

She wouldn't have married him if she hadn't.
And even though she'd asked for the divorce,
it was to save her heart from shattering any
more than it was being around him and knowing that he didn't and probably wouldn't ever
return her love.

That was why they had to move through this,
right now. Zaynab was tired of walking on egg-
shells and waiting for him to wake up and realize that he was pushing her away. Because he
was, and unless he was doing it on purpose,
and this was all some calculated ploy to chase
her out of his life, Ara was risking her really
walking away from him this time and for good.

"I am right, aren't I?" she said far more quietly. "You didn't want to be there at the party

today. And you… You don't want to be here
with me now, do you?"

When he blew a harsh breath and spun away
from her suddenly, Zaynab's heart gave a lurch.
Inhaling sharply, she squeezed her eyes shut
at the sight of him retreating, feeling a fresh
wave of new tears welling forth. Before the
overwhelming sadness warped her voice and
made it impossible for her to speak without sobbing, Zaynab sniffled and asked, "Why did you
marry me?"

Silence answered her, and so certain that
he must have walked away and left her, she
blinked open her eyes, chancing the tears that
flicked from her lashes and trailed down her
cheeks. Only to see that Ara had simply moved
a few feet away and was looking at her with this
inexplicable fury twisting his handsome face.

It was when he spoke that she understood
none of his unconcealed wrath was for her at
all, but for himself instead.

"I'm not worth your tears, Zaynab," he
growled, the rumbling of his self-directed anger
coming through clearly. "I never will be, and I
shouldn't have married you."

Zaynab sucked in a whistling breath, her
lungs burning and her vision of him blurring
with the tears now fully wetting her face.

"So Sharmarke was right when he said you

were spying on him," she said, hating to admit anything that had to do with her father, especially now that she had to accept that, like her parents, she'd failed her marriage.

"He told you that." Ara unbuttoned his suit jacket and loosened his tie, his expression far more menacing if that were possible. "He shouldn't have. It was a problem between us, him and me. There was no need for him to involve you."

"I'm your wife. His daughter. Why wouldn't it involve me? Maybe he was trying to protect me from being hurt by you." She lobbed that last part in a fit of pique, annoyed with him in part but also just devastated by their argument.

And Ara took it personally. His scowl was fierce and his eyes dark slits of irritation. "Is that what you think? That his intent was to protect you, and that you needed protection from me. That I would ever want to hurt you, Zaynab?" His big shoulders heaved and then fell, and he didn't look quite as enraged by the mention of her father when he said, "I... I have hurt you, I know, but it was never with intention. Never part of some plot to inflict pain on you. *Never.* I swear it."

Swallowing around the jagged edges of brittle emotions, Zaynab shook her head, exhausted and defeated, and knowing that pretending

Sharmarke was ever concerned for her and hadn't only been working to preserve his own reputation would be a waste of time.

This isn't about my father and what he's done wrong.

This was all her and Ara, and the wall of thorns he kept around himself, the feelings and thoughts he kept from her.

Smiling sadly, Zaynab forced herself to look at him as she blinked more tears. "You must have only married me for your cloak-and-dagger mission."

Ara couldn't believe it, but her hurled accusation was swirling in his mind, reverberating loudly as if Zaynab were uttering it over and over again.

And yet as much as it pained him to confess, there was a half-truth in what she believed of him.

"I did think that your father might be less inclined to be suspicious of me if I agreed to his suggestion of an arranged marriage." Before she could crow with triumph—not that Ara thought for a second that gloating was her aim since she looked generally stricken at his confession—and knowing that he was hurting her made the next words easier to speak in the hope she would take even the slightest comfort in them. "I did *not* know that Sharmarke meant to give his own daughter away."

"But you took the opportunity that landed in your lap anyway," she said bitingly.

She meant that he'd used her to get to her father. Hearing that she still believed that of him pulverized his confidence that she might have learned to trust him since living together again. *Why would she? I've isolated her again, and in our own home, and I made her feel this way. Made her want to lash out at me.*

The fault was entirely his and his alone.

And yet recognizing that, Ara couldn't give her what she wanted. What he could clearly see would soothe her.

Because even though it would be true if he told her that he loved her, he wasn't willing to give in to it. Refused to participate and set himself *and* Zaynab up for any future torment if their love didn't last. *Or if it was killed.*

No, he hadn't changed his mind, and after all of this, Ara was only that much more determined to keep from fully loving her and protect her from loving him.

"You're right," he said, unclenching his jaw to force out the hateful words and lying to her, "I saw an opportunity in marrying you, and I took it. I believed it was my only chance to protect the public from your father's criminal actions."

"You never loved me."

"I… No, I never loved you, not like that." The lie fell from his lips smoothly, but inside he was a writhing mass of agony. Masking it as long as possible, Ara looked away from her and delivered what he hoped was the final blow to his ongoing misery, and what he prayed made Zaynab see the light and run far, *far* away from him. "We should divorce."

He expected her to agree.

Maybe not immediately, as the quiet stretched on after he had proposed the suggestion, but eventually Zaynab would see that it was the best possible solution for her. He was a difficult husband. Unloving to her, and cruel for it, and she had always been right in her instinct to leave him.

Ara was bargaining on her still wanting the divorce, but she confused him when she asked quietly, "What did you say?"

"I'll leave. Give you the divorce, move out, but I only ask that you allow me to help you with whatever you need for the baby." Their child. Ara had wanted to be there when she gave birth, and had even once, not too long ago, secretly longed to remain by her side and watch their baby grow up with Zaynab.

Now he'd have to settle for visits and updates from her.

He could still be a good father and protect Zaynab and their child from afar.

It wasn't ideal, but it kept love out of the mix.

"I don't want a divorce."

Baffled, Ara didn't think he heard her correctly, until Zaynab made it clear that he had as her hands cradled her pregnant belly and she said, "I won't let Button grow up without a father. You owe it to be in their life."

"And I will be," he agreed vehemently.

"I know what it's like being a child of divorce." Her voice dropped an octave above a whisper, her gaze far-off, no doubt reliving the memories of hardship after Sharmarke abandoned Zaynab and her mother. "It's not easy. Questioning yourself. Rationalizing that it was somehow your fault even though it couldn't have been." She sucked in a shuddery breath, blinked and looked at him far more clearly. More than that, he noticed how she straightened her shoulders back as though preparing herself for battle. But since they were alone, her only opponent could be him.

"That's why I don't want a divorce anymore. We have to do better for our baby. Better than my father did for me."

"Zaynab, I—"

"No, Ara, listen to me. I *want* this. Need it. If you can't…" She broke off, and he knew he'd never hear what she might have said because she moved on with only the softest of hitches in her breathing, "If *we* can't make our marriage work in any traditional sense, I'm open to stay together for our baby. For Button. Please…"

Her plea broke him.

He had barely nodded when Zaynab moved toward him. Ara watched her until she was standing before him, her warmth pulling at him, and the temptation to lean into her nearly overcoming his higher reasoning.

But he also couldn't stand there any longer and withstand her dark eyes on him, her cheeks still wet from crying, and her sweet perfume infiltrating his staunch barriers.

"What are you…"

And before he could say more, she pushed her face up and pressed her lips to his. Shocked, Ara stood frozen as she kissed him. The salt of her tears mingled with the kiss, at both sweet and bitter. Though his surprise didn't last long, she didn't give him time to react, take her in his arms and return the kiss.

It was only after she pulled away that he realized why she'd done it.

"There. I think that's intimate enough to break the iddah and undo our divorce," she said, breaking his heart as she let him go. Zaynab walked around him then. And though technically he could hear her footfalls padding away, somehow Ara felt far lonelier than he had when she'd first left him in that big house of theirs in Berbera all alone.

CHAPTER THIRTEEN

ZAYNAB HAD ALWAYS thought leaving Ara would be hard, but now she knew that staying with him after learning that he didn't love her was going to be far tougher of a challenge for her.

I have to though.

For their baby's sake, she had to stay. The last thing she would wish on her own child was a distant, if not fractured relationship with their father. And despite how hollow and bereft she felt being with Ara right then, Zaynab never doubted he would be a good father. He'd keenly cared for their child from the moment she'd told him she was pregnant. He'd moved to London when she hadn't wanted to uproot her life, and he had even gifted her a lovely home as not only a dowry but to raise their child in.

It must have been why she'd thought he had a change of heart where their relationship was concerned.

I thought he cared.

More than that, Zaynab had really felt that he loved her. Clearly though she had deluded herself into seeing signs that weren't there.

And now since she had decided to remain married to him, she'd have to learn to be stony-hearted like him. Even the thought daunted her. But if it meant that Ara was more comfortable with the idea of staying married to her and not loving each other in the traditional sense, then Zaynab had to make it work somehow and some way.

It didn't help that her decision to end their divorce talk happened only about a couple days ago.

Two days in and she was already beginning to waver in her resolve and question her ability to maintain this cold front with him. It was downright exhausting to tiptoe around him, but she'd managed it. She had asked him to stop giving her rides to and from work, not wanting to be confined in the car with him if not necessary. And though they still had meals together, Zaynab no longer exerted herself in getting him to open up to her, not even when the silence that accompanied their meals only made her nervous enough to deal with indigestion all night long.

Their guests were still with them, so Zaynab at least had some company besides Ara's.

And yet Nasser and Anisa were busy touring the city and doing some shopping for their wedding, and Zaynab's mother was fully enjoying her retirement and spending time catching up with friends that she'd left behind when she had moved from London. They couldn't be with Zaynab every waking hour to keep her from thinking about Ara and what their lives might have been like had he loved her.

She was having one of those quiet, pining moments when her mother dropped in on her in her bedroom. Zaynab hadn't expected her to be back so soon, so she couldn't dash the tears away fast enough.

"Zaynab! What's the matter?" Her mother hurried to her side and hugged her. "Why are you sitting in here alone and crying?"

Zaynab looked around her, afraid that her mother's voice might have carried through the house. Anisa and Nasser were still out, but Ara was, as usual, shut up in his office. Zaynab quickly realized that she was fretting for no reason though. The chance of him having heard anything once he was absorbed in his work was merely hopeful on her part. And she also didn't have to worry about any of his security cameras catching her crying as none of the bedrooms were being monitored.

"Are you sick?" Her mother paused, her face

crumpling more with worry as she lowered her voice and asked, "Is it the baby?"

Zaynab shook her head. Though her mother heaved a sigh and whispered, "Alhamdulillah," she still clutched her chest and gazed at her uneasily.

"But if it's not the baby, and you're not sick, then what's wrong?"

Her mother was the last person she would've chosen to confide in. After surviving her battle with cancer, Zaynab had only wanted to shield her from worry, and she had for a year now. It was almost as tiring to avoid Ara as it was to keep the problems with her marriage from her mother.

Perhaps that was why she opened her mouth and blurted, "It's Ara."

And apparently that was all that needed to be said for her mother to bundle her back into her arms. Clinging to her, Zaynab buried her face in her mother's shoulder and cried more of the seemingly never-ending tears that had plagued her recently. Her mother quietly patted her back and rocked her the way she had when Zaynab was younger. When she was soothed enough to pull back and wipe at her face, Zaynab didn't see any judgment in her mother's eyes. Just the same open concern and love for her.

"Now, tell me what's wrong," her mother

urged, taking Zaynab's hands and squeezing comfort into her.

Needing to unburden herself, Zaynab told her everything. Starting with the reasons that had led her to asking Ara for a divorce and ending with her choice to remain with him in the end.

When she was done, her mother tsked. "Why didn't you tell me you were thinking of a divorce?"

"I didn't want to worry you."

Laughing, her mother gently cupped and stroked her cheek. "You will always worry me, Zaynab. Now that you will be a mother, you will understand what that feels like."

"That's why I'm staying with him. For the baby."

Her mother nodded. "I know. It's very noble of you to sacrifice for your child," she told her, her smile sympathetic.

"Is it?" Zaynab said. "It feels awful." Like her heart was breaking over and over again, and there was nothing she could do to stop it. *Because I can't make Ara love me.*

"It should since you love him."

Zaynab bit her lip, not even bothering to argue what she knew was true. She loved Ara, but that was her problem. "How do I stop?" she said pleadingly.

Her mother laughed again and smoothed her

hands over Zaynab's, lovingly caressing some of the tension from her.

"You know, I loved your father very much. And I know that, once, he cared for me too. But we grew apart, your father's heart turned away from me, and we weren't the same people who had fallen in love and chosen to be married. It's why I left him."

"You left him?" It was the first Zaynab heard of this. She'd just assumed it was her father who had wanted to separate from her mother. That it was *his* fault Zaynab's childhood wasn't what it should have been had her parents remained married.

Her mother inclined her head. "It's true. I demanded it, in fact. I sensed the end of our relationship was coming, and I wanted to beat your father to it," she said with a sad smile.

"How did you know that… Well, that you didn't love each other anymore." Although it wasn't the same for her and Ara, considering he never had loved her, Zaynab was still curious how things could have gone so wrong for her parents if what her mother was saying about their love was true.

"Besides your father saying it to me, I just looked at him one day and didn't recognize him as the man I'd loved once."

Zaynab didn't know what to say. And her

mother seemed to understand because she wrapped her in another embrace, and while holding her, she said, "It was hard, of course, and I had my moments of regret, but in the end, now more than ever, and certainly whenever I look at you, I know that leaving your father was the best decision I could've made.

"As for you and Ara, I can't choose what's best for either of you. As a mother, I want you both to be happy, even if that means living apart from each other and raising your child like that," her mother said and kissed her cheek. "Just know that I will support you in whatever decision you make, always."

It was like something clicked in her head, and Zaynab drew back, gazed into her mother's eyes, and quietly said, "I don't think I made the right decision…"

After hearing her mother loving fiercely and then bravely embracing her choice to divorce Sharmarke, Zaynab had gained a missing piece of clarity. It struck her just then that she'd never told Ara how much she cared for him, not once. She'd asked for a divorce and hadn't told him why she had been unhappy with their relationship. And now she was doing the same thing by choosing to remain quiet, staying with him and accepting a loveless marriage.

"But I think I now know how to fix it," Zaynab said to her mother, and for the first time since she and Ara had argued, she didn't have the urge to cry hopelessly.

Not for the first time, Ara had hurt Zaynab, and since it was becoming so frequent he had to accept it wasn't unintentional. Because he'd been trying to push her away for a while now with his coldly indifferent attitude. He'd closed himself off to her purposefully in the hopes that she would leave him. Spare her the grief of loving him and being committed to their relationship when he didn't think he could give her what she wanted and deserved: true love.

I would've broken her heart someday.

The way he saw it, better that the heartache and grief come earlier than having either of them be invested in each other even more.

Of course Zaynab likely didn't see it that way. Her stricken expression was branded into his memory, and even though several days had passed since she informed him that she'd changed her mind about the divorce and pleaded for them to remain married for the baby, the whole dramatic scene might as well be imprinted onto his soul. At this rate, he likely wouldn't ever forget the disappointment and heartbreak in her eyes when she'd looked at him. And he certainly wouldn't be able to scrub away the taste of her tears when she had kissed him.

Something told him that his injury to her this time might even be irreparable. That he'd well and truly broken her patience with him.

Ara just didn't think anyone else was aware of that fact until Anisa sighed and asked, "Okay. What did you do to upset Zaynab?"

They were strolling the popular shops of Notting Hill on her request. She'd wanted last-minute souvenirs and, though Nasser was free to go with her, Anisa had asked Ara specifically to come along with her. And now he knew why as she led him into a bookshop, the cool, hushed atmosphere prompting him to lower his voice as he answered her.

"What do you mean?" he said.

Turning her head away from perusing the books, Anisa raised a brow in challenge. "I mean that there's a weird tension between you two, and don't you dare try to say there isn't."

Ara closed his mouth, having planned to do exactly that. He hadn't wanted to talk about it, not only because he didn't wish to burden his sister with his relationship troubles, but also there was the fact that he didn't know how to make Zaynab happier and yet protect them both from the torment that love carried with it.

"She's *upset* with me."

"Why?" Anisa tossed back over her shoulder as she walked down the corridor of bookshelves.

She led him to the back of the shop, to a seating area with two armchairs and a sofa, the chintzy material of the furniture pairing well with the homely feeling of the bookshop. There weren't a lot of patrons in the bookshop, and so they had that area to themselves.

He must have looked confused as to how she knew about the seating area because she explained, "Nasser and I visited this bookshop yesterday." She then nudged him good-naturedly, adding, "Don't think you can change the subject. Now I know you're used to giving the advice, Ara, but I might actually be able to help you if you'll let me."

Sighing heavily, he palmed his beard and, after an anxious pause, said, "We argued."

"Is this about the divorce?"

Right. He'd almost forgotten that Anisa had overheard him speaking to Zaynab about it.

It happened when Zaynab had left him a year ago after he'd discharged himself from the hospital in Mogadishu and returned to Berbera alone. Anisa had been there waiting for him, and Nasser with her, after Ara had tasked him to guard his little sister. Though he and Anisa hadn't been on speaking terms at the time, he'd wanted her to be safe, and Nasser had proved himself capable of delivering security guarantees. And Ara had been correct in trusting his instincts and choosing Nasser to protect his sister. He just hadn't known that he was also inadvertently the reason they had met and fallen in love. Now, because of him, they were about to be married.

Meanwhile he couldn't help but be reminded that the same happiness that Nasser and Anisa shared couldn't be said of him and Zaynab.

"Yes, and no. We're not getting divorced any longer."

"So, what's the problem then?" Anisa tilted her head, her bafflement understandable. "Shouldn't we be celebrating?"

Far from feeling in a celebratory mood, Ara bowed his eyes, gripped his beard punishingly and growled, "There's no divorce, but we're only staying together for the baby."

Anisa was silent for a while, but then she snorted and said, "Well, that's stupid."

Ara jerked his head up fast, sharp and angry words forming quickly on his tongue. But before he had the chance to utter them, and deal his sister any harm, she held up a hand to stop him and acknowledged his outrage.

"I'm sorry to have been so blunt, but what I meant is that you don't have to be with each other to raise your child together."

"We know that. But Zaynab... She wants it this way." He didn't know why Zaynab would bind herself to him when Ara was giving her the chance to leave him and be free of the emotional turmoil he was causing her. And maybe, though the thought pained him greatly, she could even find happiness with someone else and be loved as wholly as she deserved.

"Did you think that this might not have to do with the baby? At least for her."

Ara went rigid, nostrils flaring and his mind turning over what Anisa had just said. "Then what would it have to do with?"

"Oh, I don't know..." She tapped her chin and rolled her eyes before giving him a sharper look than he could ever. "Could it be that, perhaps, she loves you? That she doesn't want you to end your marriage because she thinks it's her only connection to you."

He was shaking his head even before Anisa finished, unable to digest what she was insinuating. That Zaynab loved him wasn't the bombshell news here, he always knew she'd cared for him, but that she loved him to the point of accepting the passionless union he could only offer her—Ara was dumbstruck that it could be true.

"Do you love her?" Anisa asked and touched his arm and snagged his attention.

He'd been staring off into the distance, far beyond the walls of the bookshop; the shock that Zaynab's love could be so strong for him blanking his mind to any other thought. But he'd heard what Anisa had said and now he was having trouble sorting out a response.

"I… Yes." He wouldn't lie because admitting it wouldn't change that he had been right. If what Anisa proposed was true, and Zaynab's love for him was causing her torment, then Ara had reason to be worried. His fear for love hurting either of them, or even *both* of them was now real. Which was why he said, "It doesn't matter. I can't give her what she desires. I can't love her the way she should be loved."

"Why not?"

"Because," he snapped. *Because love causes untold measures of pain that ripple through life. It's a short burst of happiness that can only end in misery.* Instead of telling her all of that, he grumbled again, "Just because."

"This is about hooyo and aabo."

Hearing Anisa mention their parents only incensed him more. But he was too angry and too distraught to tell her she was wrong. *Or maybe she's right…*

Anisa didn't give him time to decide which it was. "I know what you're feeling, Ara. It might not be the same for me as it is for you. You knew them better than I did, and I was so young, that sometimes… Sometimes I can't even remember their faces it feels like." She smiled sorrowfully at him and tightened her hold on his arm. "I get so sad knowing that they won't be with me at my wedding, and they won't ever meet Nasser."

"Anisa," he rasped her name, taking her hand over his arm and squeezing her fingers.

"I want them with us so badly, it physically pains me." She looked up, breathing out slowly and fanning her face with her free hand to stave off the tears he saw glimmering in her eyes.

Instinctively, he reached for her and drew her into his arms. Anisa hugged him back as tightly as he was holding on to her. It felt like a while before they pulled apart and his sister wiped at her face, her smile wobbly but not as colored by the profound loss that changed both of their lives.

"I miss them, too," he confided, chuckling when Anisa stared wide-eyed at him. She had a right to be surprised, it wasn't often that he shared his feelings. His humor dissipated soon enough though, and with it came a hollow re- alization that Anisa was correct. At least about the part that their parents' deaths had forged his trust issues with love. If he were being honest with only himself, losing them had shaped who he was today more than he cared to admit.

And it had undoubtedly influenced his decision to keep Zaynab from getting closer now.

Though he survived his parents' passing away, Ara couldn't say the same for Zaynab. "I don't want to love and lose her. I won't survive that."

Anisa grasped his hand. "I won't say that losing her isn't possible. But what I will tell you is that when I first met Nasser, and as I gradually got to know him, I didn't know how I felt until he walked away and I allowed him to leave.

"The thing is, him leaving wasn't what I regretted most. It was my not speaking up about how it broke my heart, and I was only heartbroken because I loved him. And he felt the same way. But if Nasser and I hadn't loved each other, we wouldn't have fought to be together."

Normally Ara wouldn't have cared to hear about his sister's love life in detail, but in this instance it was illuminating.

The question though was, did he want to fight for Zaynab, their marriage and their family?

To fight for their love?

Ara seemed to have his answer when he asked Anisa, "How would I even fight for her?"

CHAPTER FOURTEEN

"ARE YOU GOING to tell me where we're going?" Zaynab asked, nervously plucking at the ruffled trim of her beige tunic before forcing her hands into the lap of her long black skirt. She glanced over at Ara as he sat behind the wheel and confidently steered through the thickest parts of London traffic. They were nearing the Thames, and it was busier than usual on that temperate spring night.

The smile lifting up a corner of his mouth should have caused her some alarm, mostly because they barely spoke to each other these days. She'd hoped to change that since speaking to her mother a couple days ago, but every time she set out to talk to Ara, she had a flash of his coldly unreadable features when he'd told her that he would sign off on their divorce and her heart froze from fear to see that look on his face again.

Despite that, now all she felt was an answering flutter when he turned his dark eyes from the road and briefly settled the force of his gaze on her. "I could, but I'd rather you see it for yourself."

She saw what he meant a short while later after they parked and walked from the footpath between the dazzling London Eye and the Thames to a pier where an impressively long boat floated gently on the dark river waters. Encased by a glass roof and walls, and lit up so brightly that it glowed, it reminded her of a giant, buoyant snow globe.

Only as they neared it Zaynab could see it wasn't a snow globe at all but a restaurant, warmly lit and redolent of polished refinement and a menu that had to be seriously pricey. But that wasn't why she hesitated halfway up the pier to the boat, looked at him warily and wondered, "Why are we here?"

It wasn't like she and Ara were on the best of speaking terms right then. Although she didn't mind the promise of dinner, Zaynab also couldn't pretend everything was normal with them either. *It's far from normal...*

She'd thought that she could remain with him and learn to be as emotionally detached in their relationship as he was, but it wasn't as easy as she presumed it to be. Worse, starving her love for him was starting to feel impossible. And it made her wonder whether she had doomed herself to forever pining away for Ara in secret, never having her love returned and never being happy with him again.

"I just wanted a change of scenery for dinner, and this restaurant came highly recommended from Anisa. Apparently she and Nasser dined here recently."

Though his explanation didn't fully settle her nerves, Zaynab nodded slowly and moved along.

At the boat, waitstaff ushered them in with smiles and guided them to one of the tables on the empty boat. Besides figuring that they arrived earlier than anyone else, she thought nothing of their being the first guests aboard the floating restaurant, except for the fact that she was now briefly stuck with Ara.

It should have been the perfect window for her to tell him how she felt about him had her tongue not anxiously tangled up on her.

I don't want a marriage that's empty of passion.

That was all she had to say, but that one sentence was full of the incomparable weight of her love for him. She couldn't just blurt it out... Could she?

Before Zaynab tried, Ara stood up from their table near the center of the boat and he left her to walk up to the glass walls of the ship.

In his well-tailored charcoal gray striped

three-piece suit, he looked the same as always. But with his back to her, his hands locked behind him, and the view of nightlife teeming along central London in front of him, Ara didn't sound like himself as he said, "Besides dinner, there's another reason I invited you here, Zaynab."

Ignoring the way her heart took a nosedive like an anchor heaved off the side of a ship and into the murky depths below, she gulped.

"I've been thinking about the divorce. About us."

She curled her hands into fists in her lap, her nails indenting into her palms.

"But before that, I have to tell you something about me. Something I hope will help you understand my reasoning and my actions lately." She heard him sigh, the sound gratingly loud in the quiet of the boat. Even the staff appeared to have made themselves scarce. And with the ship covered in glass, it truly felt like they were trapped in their own little bubble right then.

"Since my parents died, I've always carried this feeling that I should have been with them. That if I had been, I could have saved them."

Zaynab pinched her lips together and stopped the comforting words that rushed up in her, and though she forced herself to remain seated, she gazed at him with a longing to give in to the need to embrace him.

"And I might have, had I not allowed an argument to keep me away from them. I let my anger get the best of me, and although I know it didn't kill them directly, it held me back from being with them in their time of need. It's a regret I will live with for the rest of my life." She believed what he said. The grief in his voice heavy and thick, and pressing down on her lungs as though she was grieving with him. And, in a way, she was. Her love panged for him. Made her want to run up behind him and wrap her arms around his shoulders and hug him until he forgot the tragedy that both disfigured his past and shaped him into the man he was today.

She hadn't wanted to interrupt him, sensing that he needed to expunge his feelings, but Zaynab couldn't help herself from trying to console him.

"I'm sure that's not true..."

"It is," Ara intoned. Behind his back, he tightened his hands, his fingers locking around his wrist, knuckles jagged against his deep brown flesh. "Because I *should* have been there, Zaynab. I... I had time off school. A holiday break. And when most of my friends left to visit their homes, I had remained on campus to avoid the inevitable arguments I knew awaited me if I returned home to my parents. An argument about my leaving my business program and pursuing being a chef, of all things.

"It was stupid," he breathed out harshly. "And though it felt so important to me then, I wish it hadn't been. More than anything I wish—*Allah*, how I wish I had taken the time to go home, be with them, even if it was one last time."

She knew he was done when he hung his head and his shoulders drooped suddenly as if burdened by an invisible pressure. And he held perfectly still, like a beautiful statue after that, the silence no longer holding her curiosity as he'd given her a peek into what he was thinking and feeling.

But she couldn't feel relieved knowing that he was hurting.

Only before Zaynab could rise from her seat and go to him, Ara glanced at her over his shoulder.

"I hurt them with my selfishness, and I promised myself I wouldn't do that to anyone I love again. But I did, with Anisa when she moved away. Because I wanted, selfishly, to have her by my side where I could protect her. I allowed four years to pass without speaking to her, and I almost lost my remaining family because of it."

Zaynab's breathing staggered at the ardor tightening across his handsome face right before he looked away from her.

"I want to be selfish," he said, his words spoken to the glass wall in front of him, but they were aimed at her entirely. "I'm fighting against the thoughtlessness of keeping you with me. But if I lost you—Zaynab, I can't lose you. I won't. Not even if I have to act inconsiderately and make you hate me."

Hate him? The notion couldn't be further from her mind, not especially when her love for him surged up in her more powerfully than ever before.

"I loved my parents, and their deaths nearly destroyed me. If I hadn't needed to care for Anisa, needed to step up and be the remaining family she had, I don't know where I would be today. And it's because I loved them that I'm still hurting so much."

"You're right," she said, finally finding her voice and feeling like she had to speak up. "About love. I loved my father, and it pained me when I finally realized that he didn't love me back."

"It's his loss," Ara remarked.

Zaynab smiled at his quickness to defend her, not that it was needed. *Though it's appreciated.* And because she believed that she now understood where he was going with this, she said, "I know it's hard to care about someone and question if they care much back."

"I do care for you," he rasped, "love you even—"

She had already been on the edge of her seat the entire time, so she rose up fairly quickly.

"What did you say?" Walking slowly over to him, she glimpsed her reflection hovering behind him and saw the uncertainty that gripped her heart crinkling her brow and trembling her lips. She touched his shoulder when he wouldn't turn around to her, when he wouldn't repeat what he'd just told her. But that small bit of contact worked in rousing him, and Ara gave her what she wanted. What she'd always ever desired from him.

"I love you, Zaynab," he said.

"I always did," Ara said, lifting his hand to where she touched his shoulder, his palm enveloping her fingers. "That was never in doubt, at least not for me."

"I thought… You said you didn't, *couldn't.*"

"I lied."

"Why?"

"Because I didn't want you getting hurt by your father's crimes. And then because I didn't know how to be a husband to you." Telling her all of this after bottling it up inside for so long was at once terrifying and relieving. He hadn't felt freer in all his life, even though a part of

him still wanted to cower from Zaynab behind
the last shreds of his usual defenses.

I want to show her this.

He needed to at this point.

"After Sharmarke was imprisoned, I'd hoped
that maybe—" he paused and grasped her hand
a little tighter "—we could live together and I
could learn to be a better life partner to you."

"You did?"

He could see Zaynab's eyes widen in her
reflection. Although he'd finally opened the
floodgates on his thoughts and feelings, Ara
still hadn't looked at her fully. This was the
most vulnerable he'd been in a long while. Not
since his parents died and he'd equated love and
any other emotion like it as a security risk to
his mind and heart.

"I did. But then you asked for the divorce,
and I wanted to give you what you wanted. I
didn't want you to force yourself to stay with me.
When I signed the divorce application for you, I'd
thought it would be the last time I ever saw you."

Then she'd messaged him that she was pregnant, and Ara's every primal-charged instinct
was to claim his family.

"The baby was my second chance at making
amends to you," he said.

"Ara, I... I didn't know you felt that way."
She took her hand away and he let her go, but

he still didn't turn to face her, not even when he felt her stepping back away from him, her sandals moving soundlessly over the carpet. From what he could see in the glass wall's reflection, she was pacing behind him.

"At the hospital in Mogadishu, when you were in a coma, I was worried that you'd never wake up. We were married for two months then, and I was already thinking about a divorce, but then you were injured so badly and all I kept thinking was that I wouldn't speak to you again—and I knew, I just knew then that I loved you."

It wasn't news to him that she loved him. He'd begun to suspect that she did from how sad she would become because of him, but it was another thing to hear her say it aloud.

She loves me.

And she was concerned that she'd almost lost him. It was exactly the distressing kind of situation he'd wanted to avoid inflicting on her; the whole reason he had suppressed his love for her and refused to tell her of it. To think that his worst fear had already happened a while ago and that he hadn't known about it.

Ara's heart constricted, and he waited for his usual doubts to creep in and ruin this special moment with her. When nothing happened he was surprised but pleasantly so. He knew that

he owed it to Zaynab. Talking to her was helping, and had he known that it would, he might
have braved telling her all of this a while ago.

As if reading his mind, she sighed and said,
"I wish you would've told me all of this a long
time ago."

"I do too." And knowing how much he regretted it the first time Ara didn't want to suffer the remorse of another missed opportunity.
"That's why I want to ask you to give me another chance."

By his side now, Zaynab touched his hand.

"I'm scared that if I do, that it might not be
enough," Zaynab said far more quietly, the fear
threaded in her words clear to him, touching
that final part Ara hadn't even realized was
closed up in him. He hadn't looked her at her
properly when they'd been talking this whole
time. Now, desperate to remedy that, he gently
took hold of her wrist and pulled her around
him, trapping her between him and the glass
wall, and taking her face in his hands.

"I love you," he said, seeing the tears bead-
ing at her eyes and knowing that she needed to
hear it again. *That we both need it.* "I've always
loved you from the moment I first saw you. I
might have struggled to get to this point, but
Zaynab, it was never because I didn't care for
you. Never because I didn't love your heart,

your smile, everything about you that made me want to ask you to marry me."

She closed her eyes and her lips parted on a whimper.

"If you give me this chance, I swear I'll use it to show you this time." He paused, gathering his courage for this last part. "But if you can't trust me, I'll understand. I just can't give you what you've asked of me. I won't condemn us to a marriage where we're not in love."

Her eyes fluttered open at his ultimatum, a blend of a cry and laugh coming from her. "Are you saying you'll divorce me?"

"Maybe," he said, smiling stupidly as her sparkling eyes softened his heart completely.

"I don't know what to say to that."

"Say yes," he urged her and watched her chin tremble anew. Only now it wasn't because she was unhappy with him. Rather, with her eyes shining, Zaynab kept him on tenterhooks until the very last moment.

"All right," she whispered.

Ara expelled the breath he had been holding in anticipation.

"But only if you promise to speak to me. Tell me how you're feeling and let me in up here," she said, touching his temple before smiling serenely and moving her hand to his chest, her palm pressing down over his heart, "so that I know how to protect this."

Feeling his own eyes watering after that, Ara lowered his head and kissed her, giving them what he knew they both wanted and needed. Almost all too naturally, he slid his hands down to her hips and she wrapped her arms around her neck. Their kiss was at once both soft and sweet and fiercely passionate, but it was also everything in between. It was the perfect reflection of the ups and downs they'd gone through together, and now standing there, with Zaynab in his arms where she belonged all along, Ara wouldn't have had it any other way.

He would've kissed her to breathlessness just to prove his adoration for her, but they broke apart as noises filtered over to where they stood in the restaurant alone. Ara suspected that would be changing soon as the sounds crystallized into individual voices.

"I was beginning to think we might have the restaurant to ourselves," Zaynab said, her brows knitting together like the thought of sharing the space now displeased her.

"Are you disappointed that we won't?" he teased.

Still in his arms, she swatted at his chest lightly but laughed. "A little. Aren't you?"

"Oh, most definitely." Ara then bussed her

lips quickly, playfully. "But I actually rented out the restaurant for the evening."

That grabbed her attention, her face switching to confusion in the blink of an eye.

"Then who else could be here?" she asked as the noises only grew louder, the voices headed straight for them.

Ara spun her in his arms and pointed out the glass wall, his head hovering by hers, lips brushing the heated tip of her ear. "Take a look for yourself."

And she did, gasping, "Is that my mother and your sister? Salma? Oh, my God, Ara, did you invite Opaline and Remi?" She looked away from their family and friends to goggle at him. "Why?"

"Simple. They're as much a part of our lives as Button is," he said and drawing her back against him, he settled his hands over the taut swell of her belly and smiled when her hands gripped his.

She leaned into him with a little frustrated moan falling from her soft, kiss-swollen lips. "That's sweet of you, really, but I still would've liked it if it were just the two of us."

Ara laughed, never thinking he'd ever feel this lightened of burden… *Or this happy again.* With Zaynab though, he suspected he'd be happy eternally.

EPILOGUE

A few months later

IT ALL FELT full circle standing on Ara's yacht, gazing out at the horizon where the deep blue of the Indian Ocean met the cloudless blue skies of that sunny and warm late October afternoon. Zaynab didn't think there could be a more perfect day for a wedding.

Standing off at the bow by herself, she smiled at the swell of laughter and cheers sounding from behind her where Anisa and Nasser's reception was in full swing, but it was the strong arms snaking her waist from behind that had her giggling full-on. Flushed with happiness, she pushed back against Ara, knowing she'd never tire of his embraces, or stop longing for him to hold her the way he was now.

"Are you hiding from me?" he asked, nuzzling her ear and kissing her cheek.

Arching her head back and resting it on his shoulder, laughing when his lips teased along her jawline, Zaynab stroked her hands over his arms and murmured, "Maybe, but only because I know you'll have us scandalize the wedding guests."

"Not my guests," he said between little nips, "not my problem."

Zaynab snorted and let him have his way a little longer before she wriggled enough to get him to loosen his arms and allow her to turn to face him, her gaze lovingly roving over his features. She was still getting used to seeing him without that big beard of his. He'd grown it for as long as possible and then, right before she'd given birth, Ara had suddenly decided to shave it all off. Now he kept his jaw mostly clean-shaven, except for the occasional dark stubble of his five o'clock shadow.

But without the beard, the scar he'd gotten from his brush with death stood out to the world starkly.

Tracing the scar with her fingertips first, she followed it by kissing that little imperfect part of him that still, somehow, was flawless to her.

"What are you doing out here all alone?" he asked.

It must have looked strange to anyone who'd noticed her standing alone since the party was nearer the stern of the ship and spilling along the port and starboard. She had the front of the boat all to herself before Ara had sneaked up on her.

She hummed noncommittally. "Just thinking to myself, that's all."

"Are you having doubts about moving back to Berbera?"

Less than a week ago, they had settled back in his house right on time for Anisa and Nasser's wedding.

She shook her head and said, "No. Not one single doubt in my mind that we've made the right move for us."

He smiled at her and, not even bothering to see if anyone was looking in their direction, he swooped down and kissed her deeply and thoroughly. Once he ravished her into a panting, blushing state, he gestured for the shore of Batalaale Beach in the distance and where they could make out the hulking shape of the fortified stone enclosure that circled their home.

"We should head back. I miss Aasma."

"I miss her, too," Zaynab said, her heart sore at the thought of being apart from their little girl. Named in honor of Ara's late mother, little Aasma was only three months old and already she was their whole world and had them wrapped around her tiny baby fingers. "But we can't just leave your sister's wedding. What would everyone think? Besides, my mum wouldn't be too happy if we showed up early. Because then that would mean less time for her to coddle her granddaughter."

Her mother had come along to help settle them in for their new lives here. Though Zaynab was still unsure of when she and Ara and little Aasma would return to London, she was ready for it to be anywhere from a month to several years, as long as she had her family and they were all happy together.

"Though if you want to incur the wrath of your sister *and* my mother, then by all means. Just leave me out of it."

Ara mock-shuddered before grinning. "Put like that, I suppose it would only make sense for us to wait it out a little longer."

Zaynab snorted with laughter, her humor lingering but muted when he took her in his arms again, her hands wrapped around the railing of his ship, the ocean spread out before them and Ara grounding her from behind with his firm hold. "Remember when we first met."

"How could I forget?" he rumbled affectionately into her ear. "You were standing right about here and you were looking out at the ocean, gazing at the sunset. And then you turned, and looked right at me, and I knew that we were meant to be."

"Oh, did you now?" Because for a while it

had felt like they would never have made it this far. That they would never have this at all. And yet they'd persevered together, and now here they were, as happily fated as Ara believed they were.

"I did," Ara said, so solemnly that Zaynab looked back over her shoulder at him, his face right there, his lips sealing hotly over hers.

And when he moved back, his hooded gaze shifted from her mouth up to lock eyes with her. "It's because, Zaynab, I loved you from that moment onward."

If she hadn't seen that love shining back at her so openly she wouldn't have believed it.

Touching a hand to his smooth jaw, Zaynab leaned in and kissed him sweetly, injecting all the boundless joy he gave her into the gesture. Yet still not enough, she drew away and said, "I love you, too, Ara. From the moment I saw you, maybe, but certainly now and forever."

"Forever," Ara agreed resoundingly, and Zaynab had no doubt that their love would be everlasting.

* * * * *

Harlequin® Reader Service

Enjoyed your book?

Try the perfect subscription for Romance readers and get more great books like this delivered right to your door.

See why over 10+ million readers have tried Harlequin Reader Service.

Start with a Free Welcome Collection with free books and a gift—valued over $20.

Choose any series in print or ebook. See website for details and order today:

TryReaderService.com/subscriptions